*To Christopher, Martin and Elizabeth,*
*with love*

# CONTENTS

# FOREWORD

I've loved Just William for a long, long time and never in my wildest dreams did I think one day I'd be playing my childhood hero. I was about two when I first started listening to Martin Jarvis reading the Just William stories on CD, and I think the only time I ever sulked at that age was when I didn't have my CDs playing as I drifted off to sleep. Although I've always been a huge William Brown fan, it was only when my friends found out I was auditioning for the part that I realized how well known William actually is. Lots of my friends also idolized William while growing up, just as I did, along with the Outlaws (the other boys in William's gang) and all the other amazingly realistic characters Richmal Crompton created.

When I got the first audition for the BBC *Just William* adaptation, I was really excited, but there were so many other boys there I didn't think I'd get any part – least of all the role of William Brown. Then when I received the call back, it felt phenomenal. After a long series of auditions, where Paul Seed (the Director) and I simply recited the lines and chatted about rugby and dogs, I was shocked to hear that I'd been offered the part of William himself.

After a week of rehearsals (and a lot of reluctant haircuts), the other boys playing the Outlaws and I were already firm friends. I could see how many people in the script run-throughs were huge Just William fans, and also how many talented actors there were in the cast. I felt like a dwarf against giants. But the filming was really fun and everyone was so welcoming, whether we were strolling through a cornfield or eating breakfast in the Brown family's kitchen. With a great director like Paul I knew all the early mornings were definitely worth it. The filming included so many first experiences, such as filming with actors my own age, filming with animals, and I also learned to do my own stunts, which was a brilliant experience. Even Ivor, the friendly dog playing Jumble (William's scruffy mongrel), began to sink into the world of William and, after a while, followed me like his owner.

I know and love the fact that this book is going to

make so many people happy. I remember the great feeling when my mum came back from shopping with a brand-new Just William CD. William Brown is a character who will never grow old. Adults love him because they grew up with him or were just like him, and kids like me love him because he brings out the tree-climbing, pond-swimming child in all of us that can sometimes get lost in video games and cartoons. If I had the chance to switch lives with William I would do so without a care in the world, and so would many other fans. I feel so lucky to have not only acted in the series, but to have had the opportunity to play my childhood idol. I, like so many others, will never forget the Red Indian, pirate-ship captain eleven-year-old known as William Brown.

*Daniel Roche*

## CHAPTER 1

# WILLIAM GOES SHOPPING

It was the first day of the Christmas holidays, and William had spent a happy morning roaming the countryside with Ginger, Douglas and Henry. They had made fires and tracked each other through forbidden woods, they had fished in forbidden streams, and they had discussed at length that insoluble mystery—why a morning passes so much more quickly in holiday than in term time.

'Seems ext'ordin'ry to me,' said William, 'it's nearly lunch time now, an' it only seems a minute since we started out, an' in term time a mornin' always seems as long as a week. I think they do something to the clocks in holiday time,' he added darkly. 'Put 'em all on to go fast or somethin'. I don' see how it could be like that if they didn't.'

'My father's goin' to give me a watch for a Christmas present,' said Henry without much enthusiasm. 'I don't think much of watches. They always seem to come to pieces the minute you try to find out how they're made.'

'I'm goin' to buy my mother a pincushion,' said Ginger.

'I know where you can get them for twopence an' they look as if they'd cost about sixpence.'

'Oh crumbs!' said William. 'I forgot about givin' presents to people.'

'Fancy forgettin' about Christmas!' said Ginger.

'I din' forget about Christmas,' said William simply. 'I remembered about people givin' me presents. I forgot that I'd have to give 'em to people. I don't see how I can, anyway. I haven't any money.'

It turned out that William was the only one of the Outlaws who hadn't any money at all. The others had enough, with strict economy, to provide Christmas presents of a modest sort for all their families. A generous offer to give twopence each to William (which would have enabled him to purchase presents for his whole family at the Penny Bazaar) was gratefully declined.

'No thanks,' said William. 'I bet I can get money all right. I bet I'm not goin' to take your money, anyway. Thanks awfully, all the same.'

'How will you get money?' said Ginger. 'I thought you weren't gettin' any more pocket money till they'd paid for that last window you broke.'

'No, I'm not,' said William bitterly. 'I'm not, an' it seems to me window people mus' be all millionaires, the amount they charge for windows. I bet that's what I'm goin' to be when I grow up. I'm goin' to be a window maker, an' get to be a millionaire, chargin' the amount they charge for windows. An' everyone carries on as if I'd meant to break it 'stead of the ball slipping out of my hand backwards. It's jus' like 'em. Takin' all my money away an' expectin' me to give 'em Christmas presents! Still, I bet I'll get some money somehow. I bet you anything I get some money somehow. I'll weed a bed for them or somethin'.'

'There aren't any weeds in winter,' put in Ginger.

'Well, I'll do somethin' there is in winter for 'em then,' said William. 'I'll chop wood or somethin'. I bet I get some money anyway. Seems extr'ordin'ry to me that with all the money there mus' be in the world I never seem to have any . . .'

They were walking along the river bank, where some reeds grew from which William knew that whistles could be fashioned, but so far he had failed to discover the art of fashioning them. He cut several, and tried again for the hundredth time to make a whistle. As the resultant failures marked his path in a sort of trail, his spirit sank lower and lower. The whole of creation seemed leagued against him. The very reeds refused to be made into whistles by him.

The striking of the church clock reminded him that one o'clock was the hour at which his family partook of luncheon. Not wishing to prejudice his chances of money-making more than he could help, he threw away his reeds with a gesture of disgust, and ran homewards.

He had made no arrangements to meet the other Outlaws in the afternoon, because it so happened that Ginger and Douglas had to go out to tea, and Henry was going to his dancing class.

He was five minutes late for lunch, but his mother was the only other member of the family present, and her rebuke was half-hearted and mechanical. She was obviously distrait.

'William, dear,' she said. 'I'm so worried. I wonder if you'd do something for me this afternoon.'

William looked at her guardedly. 'I'm very busy this afternoon,' he said, 'it's the first afternoon of the holidays.'

As an opening move it was rather good. William had an unexpectedly delicate hand at bargaining.

'I know, dear,' said his mother, looking still more worried. 'I wouldn't ask you if I could possibly manage without.'

William assumed an expression of poignant wistfulness.

'I'd thought of goin' out with Ginger this afternoon,' he said, assuring himself as he spoke that it was the exact truth. He had thought of going out with Ginger till he heard that Ginger was being compelled reluctantly to attend a birthday party that afternoon.

'I know, dear. I hate spoiling your first day. If Ethel or Robert were home—'

William exchanged his expression of poignant wistfulness for one of shining and unselfish devotion.

'It's all right, mother,' he said. 'I'll help you any way I can.'

'That's very sweet of you, dear,' said Mrs. Brown deeply touched. 'I—I'll give you a shilling if you will.'

William felt rewarded for the muscular effort demanded by his expression of wistfulness and devotion. Without them he knew it would have been sixpence at most.

'It's this, dear,' went on his mother. 'I forgot to order the fish for dinner, and I want you to go into Hadley and get it for me.'

'Can't I get it from the village?' said William.

'No, dear. You know there isn't a fish shop in the village. You can get the half-past 'bus, and go into Hadley. You know the fish shop—Hallett's in High Street—and I'll write down on a piece of paper just what I want you to get.'

William mentally surveyed this programme. Then he said, 'Well, will you give me the shilling before I go, then I can spent it in Hadley?'

'Certainly not, dear,' said his mother. 'I shall only give you the shilling if you bring it back properly. Unless you bring it back properly I shan't give you a penny.'

The effect of his expressions of wistfulness and devotion was wearing off, and she was beginning to feel that a shilling was rather a lot for one errand.

William considered this in silence. His mind went back over his past career as an errand goer. He could not remember a single example of unqualified success.

'S'pose,' he said thoughtfully, 's'pose that I do it *nearly* all right, will you give me sixpence?'

But Mrs. Brown, who had finally come to the conclusion that a penny and his 'bus fare would have been quite enough, answered with asperity.

'Of *course* not, William. I shan't give you anything at all unless you do it perfectly, and a shilling's far too much in any case.'

'It'd save me a lot of trouble if you'd give me the shilling to spend when I've got the fish. I mean, you needn't think that I could poss'bly do anythin' wrong when it's only fish. The other times that p'raps you're thinkin' of, there were a lot of things an' I got muddled up with them, but I cudn't possibly do anythin' wrong when it's only fish. It isn't 's if I want to spend it on myself. I want to get Christmas presents for you all. I want—'

'William, do stop talking and *go!*'

William with great dignity stopped talking and went.

He walked slowly down to the 'bus terminus, and waited dejectedly. Giving up a whole afternoon and quite probably going to get nothing for it . . . Something was sure to go wrong. Something always went wrong when he was sent on errands. It wouldn't be his fault but they'd say it was. They always said it was. They'd give him the wrong change in the shop or something like that. He felt a grim certainty that he'd never see that shilling. Wasting a whole afternoon going into the town like this for nothing . . .

He took one of his abortive whistles out of his pocket and contemplated it morosely. He didn't even try to whistle it because he knew it wouldn't whistle. Everything was rotten. He was still standing staring moodily in front of him, when the 'bus came up. So sunk was he in gloomy reverie that he didn't see the 'bus till it had nearly knocked him down (he was standing in the middle of the road). The driver leant over in his seat, and gave him a short pithy résumé of his character. William, in order to restore his self-respect, leapt upon the 'bus, and had pulled the bell-rope several times before the conductor indignantly stopped him. Followed a spirited exchange of personalities with the conductor, who finally threatened to take William by the scruff of his neck and deposit him in the road outside. William, clinging to his seat, the lust of battle rising pleasantly within him, dared him to. The 'bus moved off. Whenever the conductor passed William in his duties about the 'bus, he made threatening gestures to which William responded by putting out his tongue or pulling a face. Both of them seemed to enjoy the exchange. William's spirits had risen considerably. Impossible to be depressed when a 'bus conductor had been lured from his high dignity to bandy insults with you. It was all right about that shilling. You couldn't possibly make a mistake about one errand at a fish shop. He hadn't even to remember it. His mother had written it out and put it in his pocket. To avoid any possible mistake, she'd even written it out several times and put a copy in each of his pockets. And it wasn't a question of change either, now he came to think of it. The exact money was wrapped up in paper, put into an envelope and pinned with a large safety pin into his jacket pocket. Certainly it was not going to be Mrs. Brown's fault if anything went wrong . . . And considering the matter with rising spirits, William didn't see how anything possibly could go wrong. Hurling his most hideously contorted grimace at the conductor in answer to his shaken fist, and seeing the whole world flooded with a rosy light, he felt as sure of that shilling as if he held it in his hand. Even the whistles, he felt certain, would whistle with a very little more cutting . . .

The 'bus stopped at the top of the hill leading into Hadley. William preferred to get out here rather than to go on to High Street, because he knew that there was a half-built house near the top of the hill, and William loved half-built houses. He rang the 'bus bell seven or eight times in swift succession, dodged a well-aimed box on the ear from the conductor, and leapt to the ground. Having reached it, he stood and exchanged verbal hostilities with the conductor till the 'bus was out of sight. Then he turned his attention to the house. He had climbed up the scaffolding and walked several times backwards and forwards across a narrow plank that joined two unfinished walls, before one of the workmen discovered him and sent him about his business. He had only just time to snatch a piece of putty from another workman in his headlong flight. A piece of hard cement caught him neatly on the ear as he fled. Having got out of range, he sat down on the roadside to experiment with his piece of putty. He made it into all the shapes he could think of, then put it in his pocket and sauntered on down the road. No need, of course, to hurry. There was only the fish to get, and he needn't be back before tea time. He took up his whistle and his penknife again, and began to cut the hole a little wider. Perhaps that was what was wrong. He blew . . . not a sound. He felt suddenly that life would hold no more savour for him if he couldn't find out how to make whistles. Suddenly he heard a voice behind him.

'An' what are ye tryin' to do, young sir?'

He turned round.

An old man sat on a chair outside a cottage door. So intent had William been upon putty and his whistle that he had not noticed him before.

'Make a whistle,' he said shortly and returned to his attempts.

'It's the wrong way,' quavered the old man. 'Ye'll never make a whistle that way.'

William wheeled round, open-mouthed. 'D'you know how to make a whistle?' he said breathlessly.

'Ay. Course I do,' said the old man. 'Course I do. I were the best hand at makin' a whistle for miles when I were your age. Let's look at it now . . . let's look at it.'

He inspected William's abortive attempt at whistle-making with unconcealed contempt.

'Ye'll never make a whistle this way. Never, never. Where's your sense, boy? Where's your sense?'

The 'bus conductor would have been amazed at William's humility before this master of his craft.

'I dunno,' said William. 'I—I sort of thought that was how you did it.'

'Tch! Tch!' said the old man testily. 'What on earth are boys coming to? How old are you?'

'Eleven.'

'Eleven an' can't make a whistle! I'd 'a' bin ashamed at your age! I would for sure.'

William received all this meekly, only saying at the end:

'Could you show me how to do it?'

'How can I!' said the old man irritably, 'now you've cut it about like this? How could anyone make a whistle o' this? You'll have to get me another reed. Quickly.'

'I don't know where there are any,' said William.

'Tch! Tch!' said the old man. 'Fancy not knowing where there are any. At your age. I don't know what boys are coming to, I don't. Through that stile, across the field, down to the river. You'll find them growing by the river. Why, when I was a boy—'

But William had already vaulted the stile, and was half-way across the field. He returned panting a few minutes later with an armful of reeds. The old man was waiting for him with his penknife. William handed him a reed, and he began to cut it at once, as earnest and intent as William himself.

'This way . . . an' then that . . . don' make the hole too big . . . I wish I'd got my ole Dad's penknife. An' I *ought* to have it by rights, too.'

'Now, Dad,' said a woman's voice from inside the cottage. 'Don't start on that again.'

'All very well sayin' don' start on that again,' said the old man. 'All very well sayin' that . . . mind you cut enough away here . . . I *ought* to have my ole Dad's penknife by rights. He'd promised it me an' he left it to me in his will. Charlie always wanted it too, but my ole Dad he promised it to me an' left it to me in his will.'

A middle-aged woman came to the cottage door to continue the discussion.

'Yes, he left it to you in his will and you lost it.'

'I did *not* lose it,' said the old man, beginning to shape another whistle. 'I lent it to Charlie an' he never give it me back.'

'He says he did an' you lost it.'

'It's only me 'n' you he says that to,' said the old man. 'Others have seen it up there behind his shop. He keeps it on his desk. Makes a joke of it to 'em. He says I can have it if I'll come for it. If I'd got the use of my legs . . .'

'I'm sick of hearing about the penknife,' said the woman. 'What do you want with penknives at your age?'

'What's age got to do with it? You tell me any age a man doesn't want a good penknife while he's above ground! Ever since I was a nipper I wanted that penknife of Dad's. They don' make penknives like that nowadays. You can't buy 'em for money. Charlie always wanted it too, but Dad he always said I could have it. He left Charlie his watch, but he left me his penknife.'

'Well, you got it, din't you?' said the woman.

'Ay. I got it, but Charlie'd had his eye on it all those years, an' he borrowed it an' never give it me back.'

The woman sighed impatiently.

'He gave it you back an' you lost it. He told me so.'

'Ay. He told you so. Well, he's told others different. An' they've seed it. It's on his desk in the room back of the shop. He told 'em that he'd always meant to have that penknife an' that I can have it back if I'll go for it, me that's lost the use of my legs this twelve-months and more. I tell you that penknife—'

'I'm sick to death of hearing about that penknife,' said the woman and went back into the cottage, slamming the door.

The old man had been whittling away at another whistle as he talked. He went on talking and whittling.

'You don' find any knives like my old Dad's now. A great big one of horn with his 'nitials on. Made in the days when a penknife was a penknife. Over an' over again's the time my old Dad told us that Charlie was to have his watch an' me his knife. I might've known that Charlie'd get both in the end. Like that he was as a boy an' a man don't change his nature. Waits till I've lost the use of my legs an' then borrers it an' never gives it me back. Always like that, he was. From a boy. Cunnin' an' bidin' his time. If I'd got the use of me legs he wouldn't have dared. I'd've gone up to his place an' had it off him . . . Now have a blow at that an' see if it's all right.'

William had a blow. It was all right, so much all right that the woman shut the window with a bang, saying that she couldn't stand it and an old man like him ought to know better. The old man was highly delighted by this, and, taking the whistle from William, blew it several times, chuckling to himself between the blasts.

'Now you make one all yourself,' he said to William.

He watched as eagerly as if the fate of both of them depended upon the result. When finally William, almost trembling with suspense, raised the whistle to his lips and blew a shrill blast, he clapped his gnarled hands and chuckled again.

'Fine!' he said. 'Fine! Now, that's a proper whistle, that is. Shameful—warn't it?—to think of a boy of your age not being able to make a whistle. Hundreds of them I've made, hundreds, with my old Dad's knife when I was a boy. If I'd got my old Dad's knife—when I think of that Charlie havin' it—well, it keeps me awake at night, it does . . .'

'FINE!' SAID THE OLD MAN. 'NOW, THAT'S A PROPER WHISTLE, THAT IS.'

'Where does he live?' asked William.

'Got a little tobacconist's in High Street next the boys' outfitters. I've never been down there since he took it. If I'd got the use of my legs—well, now you can make a whistle, can't you?'

'Yes,' said William and blew another piercing blast.

The woman came out of the cottage, and addressed William irritably.

'I'm sick of that noise,' she said. 'Get off with you! He's trouble enough alone, but when he gets with the likes of you . . .'

The old man chuckled.

'You'd better be goin',' he said to William. He glanced at the basket. 'Shoppin' for your ma, I reckon?'

'Yes,' said William.

'Mind you take back the right change . . . Blow again an' make sure it's all right.'

William blew again.

'Be off with you!' said the woman.

The old man chuckled.

'Thanks awfully,' said William to the old man, and, seeing the woman advancing threateningly upon him, hastily departed.

He walked up the road to High Street as light-heartedly as if he trod air. He *did* tread air. He was in the seventh heaven of pride and rapture. He could make whistles. He saw himself in the future making hundreds and hundreds and hundreds of whistles. Life seemed all too short for the whistles he meant to make. He'd teach Ginger and

Douglas and Henry. They'd all make whistles . . .

And together with the pride and rapture, his heart overflowed with gratitude to his benefactor—the marvellous old man who had taught him how to make whistles.

Now gratitude with William was not a passive quality but an active one. When William felt grateful to anyone, his spirit knew no rest till he had expressed that gratitude in action. And he felt so grateful to the old man that his gratitude was as if it were a balloon blown up inside him so taut that soon it must burst, and he with it, unless the pressure were relieved by action. His old Dad's penknife . . . William slackened his pace, and began to examine the shops he passed. A tobacconist's, and next door to it a boys' outfitters. There couldn't be any mistake about that. William stood still, and gazed cautiously about him. An afternoon drowsiness possessed the little street. No one was passing. The shops all seemed asleep. He peered into the tobacconist's shop. It was empty of shopkeeper and customers alike. He tiptoed into it, prepared to demand a cigarette card, then if necessary fly for his life should anyone come forward from the inner room to accost him. But no one came. Summoning all his courage, he tiptoed to the doorway of the inner room and looked about. It was empty. In the corner by the window was an old-fashioned desk. On it was a pen tray and on the pen tray was a pen, a pencil and—an enormous ancient horn penknife. William's eyes gleamed. He darted forward, seized it, then turned to run back to the road. But unfortunately in his haste he overturned a chair. He heard an angry shout behind him, and knew that someone had come running down a small flight of stairs at the sound and had caught sight of his vanishing figure. He leapt through the shop to the street, and cast a lightning glance up and down. It was a long street without any side turnings. His pursuer was so near him now that there was no doubt at all of his capture if he ran in either direction. The door of the boys' outfitting shop next door was open. William plunged into it. A bald-headed man was fast asleep in a basket chair behind the counter. William's entry roused him. He stirred. The chair creaked. He was obviously about to open his eyes. William looked about him desperately. There wasn't a fraction of an inch of hiding place in the shop. Without stopping to consider, William pulled aside a curtain and leapt into the window where stood a row of wax models about his own size wearing tweed suits. He snatched a label 'Latest Fashion 63*s*.' from the nearest, pinned it on to his own suit, and took his place at the end of the row. Immediately afterwards, just as the bald-headed man was opening his eyes and looking about him in a bewildered fashion, a short stout man plunged through the doorway.

The bald-headed man looked at him sternly. It was evident that he put down to his entry the noise that had roused him from his slumbers.

'What on earth's the matter?' he said indignantly. 'Anyone would think the place was on fire.'

'A boy,' panted the stout man. 'In my shop . . . in my back room . . . chased him out . . . came in here . . .'

The bald-headed man looked about him.

'Nonsense!' he said. 'No boy's been in here.'

'I saw him. I tell you, I *saw* him.'

The bald-headed man was rather annoyed.

'Very well. Find him, then. See if you can find him. I've seen no boys.'

The stout man began to examine the shop, peering into corners and crevices that could not possibly contain a boy, opening cupboards and even drawers.

'Well, have you found him?' said the bald-headed man sarcastically.

'He probably slipped past you into the back room. He did that with me. That was where I found him.'

'Did he take anything?'

'I don't know. I've not had time to find out. I

just saw him and ran after him.'

'All right. Look in the back room if you think he's there,' said the bald-headed man. He'd been awakened too suddenly, and was still feeling irritable. 'Look all over the house if you want to. Why don't you accuse me of harbouring thieves right out?'

'Oh nonsense,' said the stout man, 'but he broke into my house and I want to bring him to justice.'

With that he went into the inner room, and later could be heard upstairs searching the bedroom.

William stood in the window with the row of models, holding his breath, his heart in his mouth. Several people had passed outside, but no one had happened to look into the window.

The stout man came downstairs.

'No,' he said, 'he doesn't seem to be anywhere about here . . .'

'Are you sure he came in here at all?' said the bald-headed man.

The other was obviously rather disconcerted by his failure to find the culprit.

'I could swear he did,' he said, but he spoke rather uncertainly.

'Well, I could swear he didn't,' said the boys' outfitter. 'He probably went next door, and he'll have got off safe and sound while you've been wasting your time here. I don't believe there ever was a boy. You fell asleep and had a nightmare . . .'

But the other had already gone next door—a sweet shop with little tables for the consumption of ice cream and lemonade.

He returned excitedly a few seconds later.

'A boy *did* go in there,' he said. 'Just about the time it would have been. He bought a pennyworth of sweets, and then went away. He must have just given me the slip by doing that. I'm going to ring up the police. I'm going to ring up the police at once.' With that he turned, and hastened out of the shop.

The boys' outfitter cluck-clucked with annoyed contempt, muttered 'What a fuss! What a fuss! He must have dreamed it!' put on his spectacles, took out a ledger, drew his chair up to the counter, and began to study it. William, still standing to attention among the row of models, was beginning to feel more and more ill at ease each second. At first it had seemed to him as if he had gloriously saved the situation, but he was realising that the situation was by no means saved, that the dénouement was merely postponed and might be doubly horrible, as he would now, when discovered, have a second enemy in the bald-headed man whose window he at present adorned.

He could see no possible way of avoiding it. The bald-headed man was fully awake now, and sat barring his only way of escape. At any minute he might be discovered. He had taken advantage of the fluster of the entry of Charlie, to seize a straw hat from the floor near him and put it on his head, dragging it down far over his eyes. It certainly helped to cover his face, but it rather drew attention to his figure than otherwise, because it was so much too big for him. The mid-day hush was lifting from the little street. Shoppers were appearing. They passed the shop in twos or threes, talking, paying little attention, fortunately, to the models in the boys' outfitter's window. William scanned them fearfully from beneath the brim of his large straw hat, standing very, very still, trying not to breathe. One woman, who held a little girl by the hand, stopped and looked at the models attentively. A ventilator at the top of the window was open, and William could hear their comments.

'Well,' she said at last, 'I don't think much of the suit the end one's got on, do you, Ermyntrude?'

'Naw,' said the little girl.

'I may be short sighted, but it's not a suit *I'd* like to pay sixty-three shillings for. Looks a proper bad shape to me. *And* knocked about. And if the boots and stockin's go with it, I don't think much of 'em, do you, Ermyntrude?'

'Naw,' said Ermyntrude. 'And it's 'at's too big for it too.'

'Not what they used to be—none of these shops.'

Ermyntrude was bending down in order to see under the large brim.

'It's gotter nugly face too,' she commented dispassionately.

'Well, they can't 'elp their faces,' said the woman. 'They make 'em with wax out of a sort of mould, and when the mould gets old the faces begin to come out queer. An' sometimes they get a bit pushed out of shape.'

'This one's mould was old,' said Ermyntrude with interest, 'an' pushed out of shape, too, I should think.'

'Yes, I 'ates wax figures in any case. Unnatural I calls 'em. But if they've got to 'ave them they needn't 'ave them lookin' like nightmares wearin' clothes that look fit for a rummage stall. None of them shops are anythin' like as good as they used to be when I was a girl. Come on, love. We'll never get the shoppin' done at this rate.'

They passed on. William heaved a sigh of relief—a relief that was tempered with indignation at the strictures that had been passed upon his appearance. It had needed a superhuman effort to refrain from pulling his most diabolical face at Ermyntrude from beneath his hat. The hat was becoming something of a problem. It had slipped

ERMYNTRUDE BENT DOWN TO SEE UNDER THE LARGE BRIM. 'IT'S GOT AN UGLY FACE, TOO,' SHE COMMENTED.

WILLIAM SCANNED THEM FEARFULLY, TRYING NOT TO BREATHE. HE COULD HEAR THEIR COMMENTS.

forward over his nose so that he had to tilt his face up to keep it on. He dared not raise his hand to put it back, and he was afraid every minute of its falling forward over his face on to the floor and precipitating the crisis. While he was wondering whether he dared to adjust it with a lightning movement of his hand, he discovered that some more spectators had arrived. Half a dozen small boys were flattening their noses against the glass and gazing at the wax models. William realised with relief that their attention was not concentrated on him. They were in fact gazing at the other models.

'They're dead boys,' one of them was saying in low fearful tones. 'I know they're dead boys. My brother told me. The shop-man goes out after dark catchin' 'em. Then when he's killed 'em he dresses 'em up and puts 'em in his shop window. If you was to come past his shop after dark he'd get you. My brother said so. My brother once met him after dark carryin' a sack over his shoulder . . .'

The proprietor caught sight of the row of them flattening their noses against his glass, and ran out of his shop to scatter them. He returned to his ledger muttering indignantly. The was figures were a recent purchase. He'd never had them before, and they were the only ones of their kind in the little town. He was very proud of them, but they had attracted so much attention from the juvenile population that he was beginning to resent it. He was tired of seeing crowds of boys hanging about his shop window. He was tired of being asked—from a safe distance—if he was looking for another boy. The rumour had been invented by the older boys as a joke, but it was taken quite seriously by many of the smaller ones, and the proprietor from being amused had come to be irritated.

'Ridic'lous nonsense!' he muttered to his ledger, 'ridic'lous nonsense! Never came across such ridic'lous nonsense!' The dispersed group of boys was gradually and cautiously reassembling, and now stood in full force again flattening its noses against the glass and gazing with awe and horror at the wax figure.

'That one'd be just about your age, George—got hair like yours too.'

'Are those the clothes he found 'em wearing?'

'No. He puts new clothes on 'em.'

Suddenly the smallest boy gave a scream of excitement.

'*Oo!* Look! Look at the one at the end, the one with the hat. He forgot to put new clothes on that one. It's got its old ones on.'

They contemplated William in tense silence. Then the smallest one, who was evidently the most observant, gave another scream of excitement.

'It's *breathin'*. Watch it! It's *breathin'!* It's not dead.'

They gazed at this phenomenon, open-mouthed, open-eyed. William, though trying to retain immobility and to cease breathing, found the spectacle of their noses flattened to whiteness against the glass irresistibly fascinating. Every now and then one of them would wipe away the film of breath from the glass with a sweep of his arm in order to gain a more uninterrupted view. They gazed at him with fascinated horror.

'Look!' said the smallest one again, craning his head to look under the hat. 'It's movin' its eyes too. I can see it movin' its eyes. It's comin' alive! It's coming alive! They do sometimes. Moths do sometimes after you've put 'em in a killin' bottle.'

'Go an' tell him it's comin' alive,' said another.

'*You* go'n tell 'im.'

At this moment the hat slid forward. Instinctively William caught it and replaced it on his head. Seeing that the situation was completely lost, he relieved his feelings by pulling his most hideous face at the row of gaping spectators, and then put out his tongue.

'*Oo!* G'n, tell him quick. It's come alive. It'll get away in a minute. Tell him to come quick.'

Their sympathies seemed to have unexpectedly

veered round to the shop-owner.

The smallest boy put his head into the shop, and called out excitedly.

'I say, mister! One of them boys in the window's comin' alive—'

With a roar of fury the proprietor rushed out after them. They fled before him down the street. Seizing his opportunity, William leapt from the window out of the shop, and sped up the road like an arrow from a bow. A second and more furious bellow of rage behind him told him that the proprietor had seen him, and had diverted his pursuit to him. He fled breathlessly up the hill and round the group of cottages. The old man still sat outside his cottage door. William flung him the penknife as he passed without even stopping to see if his pursuer were still on his track. The old man's voice followed him on his headlong flight.

'Me old Dad's penknife! Glory be! Me old Dad's penknife!'

The 'bus was waiting at the top of the hill. William leapt upon it just as it started off, not turning to look behind him till he was safe in its shelter. No one was in sight. The proprietor of the shop had evidently given up the chase. William glanced about him. It was the same conductor as on his former journey. His face had brightened as William entered.

'Hello!' he said. 'I never thought they'd let you come back.'

'Why not?' said William.

'There's a circus down at Hadley with performing monkeys. I thought they'd have kept you for that.'

William replied breathlessly but with spirit:

'Oh no. They said they weren't doin' much business. The people in Hadley'd seen you so often that the performin' monkeys seemed quite or'din'ry.'

With such conversation they zestfully beguiled the journey till they reached William's stopping place. There the conductor made playful feints of kicking him off the 'bus, to which William responded by a whirlwind display of fists. The conductor watched his disappearing figure wistfully as the 'bus went on its journey. The only other passengers were a septuagenarian clergyman, and a tall angular woman who had already reproved him for giving her a dirty sixpence among her change. William walked on jauntily homewards. He'd had a jolly exciting afternoon, and he'd learnt how to make whistles. He took from his pocket the whistle that he'd made, and raising it to his lips drew a piercing blast. His heart swelled with pride. It was every bit as good as the one the old man had made. He'd got that too somewhere in another pocket. He put in his hand for it. His hand encountered a mysterious envelope with something hard inside. It was pinned. William unpinned it, took it out and opened it. Money. He stood gazing at it with an expression of mystification. Money. What on earth— And then suddenly he'd remembered. Hallett's. The fish. The errand he'd gone into Hadley for. He hadn't once thought of it since the moment he'd boarded the 'bus to go into Hadley. The shilling. He'd been going to have a shilling for it. A shilling to buy Christmas presents for his family. It was too late to go back to Hadley now. And he hadn't any money to go back with even if it weren't. He'd spent the money his mother had given him for his 'bus fare, and if he used the money she'd given him for the fish he couldn't buy the fish. It was rotten. He wouldn't get that shilling and everyone would be mad about it. They'd go on and on and *on* at him. Expecting a person to remember *everything* like that. How could a person remember *everything*? All the excitement of the afternoon had faded. He remembered the whistles, but the thrill had faded even from the whistles. He couldn't give all his family whistles for Christmas presents. He wouldn't even have time for teaching his glorious new craft to the other Outlaws. He'd have to spend all his time between now and Christmas performing menial tasks for his family in order to earn enough money to buy Christmas presents for them. William suspected (not for the first time) that Christmas was an overrated festival.

He walked slowly and apprehensively up the garden path, steeling himself to meet his mother's reproaches. He even searched round for possible excuses but found none. The idea of pretending to have acted from humanitarian principles because he thought it wrong to kill fishes occurred to him, but was dismissed as untenable in view of the fact that he spent the larger part of his holidays angling for fish in the village stream with a bent pin on the end of a string.

He entered the house slowly with a sinking heart.

His mother came out of the drawing-room.

'Oh, William darling, I'm *so* sorry. I *quite* forgot that Hallett's closed this afternoon,' went on Mrs. Brown. 'It's *so* stupid of them to have a different closing afternoon from the other shops. I remembered as soon as you'd gone.'

William tried to assume the expression of one who had gone on an errand to a shop and found it closed. 'Did you feel very cross with me, darling?' went on his mother.

'No,' said William sweetly. 'No, not at all, mother.'

'I felt so much annoyed with myself because I think nothing's so annoying as a fruitless journey and I know you hate going into the town. We're going to have omelettes instead of fish so it's all right. I'm afraid you had a very dull afternoon.'

'It's all right,' said William with an expression of suffering patience, 'it's quite all right, mother.'

'You've brought the money back?'

He handed her the money.

'You can have the shilling, of course, dear, just as if you'd done it, because it was only the accident of the shop being closed that prevented you. *And* another sixpence because it must have been so annoying for you.'

William swaggered down the road, his whistle at his lips, emitting blasts with every breath. One hand was in his pocket, lovingly fingering his shilling and his sixpence. He'd go to the Penny Bazaar and buy his presents first and then *that'd* be over, and no one would be able to talk about ingratitude and things like that, and, if they didn't like the presents he bought them, they could jolly well do without. They wouldn't be able to say he hadn't bought them any anyway. And he ought to have a good lot over because he wasn't going to spend more than he could help on their presents. Everyone said that it was the *thought* that mattered not the actual value of the present so he'd jolly well take them at their word. Then he'd meet the other Outlaws and teach them how to make whistles. Life seemed to stretch before him—one long glorious opportunity for whistle making.

He gathered breath and blew a piercing blast—a pæan of exultation and triumph and joy of life.

CHAPTER 2

# WILLIAM AND THE SCHOOL REPORT

It was the last day of term. The school had broken up, and William was making his slow and thoughtful way homeward. A casual observer would have thought that William alone among the leaping, hurrying crowd was a true student, that William alone regretted the four weeks of enforced idleness that lay before him. He walked draggingly and as if reluctantly, his brow heavily furrowed, his eyes fixed on the ground. But it was not the thought of the four weeks of holiday that was worrying William. It was a suspicion, amounting almost to a certainty, that he wasn't going to have the four weeks of holiday.

The whole trouble had begun with William's headmaster—a man who was in William's eyes a blend of Nero and Judge Jeffreys and the Spanish Inquisitioners, but who was in reality a harmless inoffensive man, anxious to do his duty to the youth entrusted to his care. William's father had happened to meet him in the train going up to town, and had asked him how William was getting on. The headmaster had replied truthfully and sadly that William didn't seem to be getting on at all. He hadn't, he said, the true scholar's zest for knowledge, his writing was atrocious and he didn't seem able to spell the simplest word or do the simplest sum. Then, brightening, he suggested that William should have coaching during the holidays. Mr. Parkinson, one of the Junior form masters who lived near the school, would be at home for the four weeks, and had offered to coach backward boys. An hour a day. It would do William, said the headmaster enthusiastically, all the good in the world. Give him, as it were, an entirely new start. Nothing like individual coaching. Nothing at all. William's father was impressed. He saw four peaceful weeks during which William, daily occupied with his hour of coaching and its complement of homework, would lack both time and spirit to spread around him that devastation that usually marked the weeks of the holiday. He thanked the headmaster profusely, and said that he would let him know definitely later on.

William, on being confronted with the suggestion, was at first speechless with horror. When he found speech it was in the nature of a passionate appeal to all the powers of justice and fair dealing.

'In the *holidays*,' he exclaimed wildly. 'There's *lors* against it. I'm sure there's *lors* against it. I've never heard of *anyone* having lessons in the holidays. Not *anyone!* I bet even *slaves* didn't have lessons in the holidays. I bet if they knew about it in Parliament, there'd be an inquest about it. Besides I shall only get ill with overworkin' an' get brain fever same as they do in books, an' then you'll have to pay doctors' bills an' p'raps,' darkly, 'you'll have to pay for my funeral too. I don't see how *anyone* could go on workin' like that for months an' *months* without ever stoppin' once an' not get brain fever and die of it. Anyone'd think you *wanted* me to die. An' if I did die I shun't be surprised if the judge did something to you about it.'

His father, unmoved by this dark hint, replied, coolly, 'I'm quite willing to risk it.'

'An' I don't like Mr. Parkinson,' went on William gloomily, 'he's always cross.'

'Perhaps I can arrange it with one of the others,' said Mr. Brown.

'I don't like any of them,' said William, still more gloomily, 'they're all always cross.'

He contemplated his wrongs in silence for a few minutes, then burst out again passionately:

''T'isn't as if you weren't makin' me pay for that window. It's not fair payin' for it *an'* havin' lessons in the holidays.'

'It's nothing to do with the window,' explained Mr. Brown wearily.

'I bet it is,' said William darkly. 'What else is it if it's not for the window? I've not done anythin' else lately.'

'It's because your work at school fails to reach a high scholastic standard,' said Mr. Brown in a tone of ironical politeness.

'How d'you know?' said William after a moment's thought. 'How d'you know it does? You've not seen my report. We don't get 'em till the last day.'

'Your headmaster told me so.'

'Ole Markie?' said William. 'Well,' indignantly, 'I like that. I *like* that. He doesn't teach me at all. He doesn't teach me anythin' at all. I bet he was jus' makin' it up for somethin' to say you. He'd got to say somethin' an' he couldn't think of anythin' else to say. I bet he tells everyone he meets that their son isn't doing well at school jus' for somethin' to say. I bet he's got a sort of habit of saying it to everyone he meets an' does it without thinkin'.'

'All right,' said William's father firmly, 'I'll make no arrangements till I've seen your report. If it's a better one than it usually is, of course, you needn't have coaching.'

William felt relieved. There were four weeks before the end of the term. Anything might happen. His father might forget about it altogether. Mr. Parkinson might develop some infectious disease. It was even possible, though William did not contemplate the possibility with any confidence, that his report might be better. He carefully avoided any reference to the holidays in his father's hearing. He watched Mr. Parkinson narrowly for any signs of incipient illness, rejoicing hilariously one morning when Mr. Parkinson appeared with what seemed at first to be a rash but turned out on closer inspection to be shaving cuts. He even made spasmodic effort to display intelligence and interest in class, but his motive in asking questions was misunderstood, and taken to be his usual one of entertaining his friends or holding up the course of the lesson, and he relapsed into his usual state of boredom, lightened by surreptitious games with Ginger. And now the last day of the term had come, and the prospect of holiday coaching loomed ominously ahead. His father had not forgotten. Only last night he had reminded William that it depended on his report whether or not he was to have lessons in the holidays. Mr. Parkinson looked almost revoltingly healthy, and in his pocket William carried the worst report he had ever had. Disregarding (in common with the whole school) the headmaster's injunction to give the report to his parents without looking at it first, he had read it apprehensively in the cloak-room and it had justified his blackest fears.

He had had wild notions of altering it. The word 'poor' could, he thought, easily be changed to 'good', but few of the remarks stopped at 'poor', and such additions as 'Seems to take no interest at all in this subject' and 'Work consistently ill prepared' would read rather oddly after the comment 'good.'

William walked slowly and draggingly. His father would demand the report, and at once make arrangements for the holiday coaching. The four weeks of the holidays stretched—an arid desert—before him.

'But one hour a day can't spoil the whole holidays, William,' his mother had said, 'you can surely spare one hour out of twelve to improving your mind.'

William had retorted that for one thing his mind didn't need improving, and anyway it was *his* mind and he was quite content with it as it was, and for another, one hour a day *could* spoil the whole holidays.

'It can spoil it *absolutely*,' he had protested. 'It'll just make every single day of it taste of school. I shan't be able to enjoy myself any of the rest of the day after an hour of ole Parkie an' sums an' things. It'll spoil every *minute* of it.'

'Well, dear,' Mrs. Brown had said with a sigh, 'I'm sorry, but your father's made up his mind.'

William's thoughts turned morosely to that conversation

as he fingered the long envelope in his pocket. There didn't seem to be any escape. If he destroyed the report and pretended that he had lost it, his father would only write to the school for another, and they'd probably make the next one even more damning to pay him out for giving them extra trouble. The only possibility of escape was for him to have some serious illness, and that, William realised gloomily, would be as bad as the coaching.

To make things worse an aunt of his father's (whom William had not seen for several years) was coming over for the day, and William considered that his family was always more difficult to deal with when there were visitors. Having reached the road in which his home was, he halted irresolute. His father was probably coming home for lunch because of the aunt. He might be at home now. The moment when the report should be demanded was, in William's opinion, a moment to be postponed as far as possible. He needn't go home just yet. He turned aside into a wood, and wandered on aimlessly, still sunk in gloomy meditation, dragging his toes in the leaves.

'If ever I get into Parliament,' he muttered fiercely, 'I'll pass a *lor* against reports.'

He turned a bend in the path and came face to face with an old lady. William felt outraged by the sight of her—old ladies had no right to be in woods—and was about to pass her hurriedly when she accosted him.

'I'm afraid I've lost my way, little boy,' she said breathlessly. 'I was directed to take a short cut from the station to the village through the wood, and I think I must have made a mistake.'

William looked at her in disgust. She was nearly half a mile from the path that was a short cut from the station to the village.

'What part of the village d'you want to get to?' he said curtly.

'Mr. Brown's house,' said the old lady, 'I'm expected there for lunch.'

The horrible truth struck William. This was his father's aunt, who was coming over for the day. He was about to give her hasty directions, and turn to flee from her, when he saw that she was peering at him with an expression of delighted recognition.

'But it's William,' she said. 'I remember you quite well. I'm your Aunt Augusta. What a good thing I happened to meet you, dear! You can take me home with you.'

William was disconcerted for a moment. They were in reality only a very short distance from his home. A path led from the part of the wood where they were across a field to the road where the Browns' house stood. But it was no part of William's plan to return home at once.

He'd decided to put off his return as far as possible, and he wasn't going to upset his arrangements for the sake of anyone's aunt, much less his father's.

He considered the matter in frowning silence for a minute, then said:

'All right. You c'n come along with me.'

'Thank you, my dear boy,' said the old lady brightening. 'Thank you. That will be *very* nice. I shall quite enjoy having a little talk with you. It's several years since I met you, but, of course, I recognised you at once.'

William shot a suspicious glance at her, but it was evident that she intended no personal insult. She was smiling at him benignly.

She discoursed brightly as William led her further and further into the heart of the wood and away from his home. She told him stories of her far off childhood, describing in great detail her industry and obedience and perseverance and love of study. She had evidently been a shining example to all her contemporaries.

'There's no joy like the joy of duty done, dear boy,' she said. 'I'm sure that *you* know that.'

'Uh-huh,' said William shortly.

As they proceeded on into the wood, however, she grew silent and rather breathless.

'Are we—nearly there, dear boy?' she said.

They had almost reached the end of the wood, and another few minutes would have brought them out into the main road, where a 'bus would take them to within a few yards of William's home. William still had no intention of going home, and he felt a fierce resentment against his companion. Her chatter had prevented his giving his whole mind to the problem that confronted him. He felt sure that there was a solution if only he could think of it.

He sat down abruptly on a fallen tree and said casually:

'I'm afraid we're lost. We must've took the wrong turning. This wood goes on for miles an' miles. People've sometimes been lost for days.'

'With—with no food?' said Aunt Augusta faintly.

'Yes, with no food.'

'B-but, they must have died surely?'

'Yes,' said William, 'quite a lot of 'em were dead when they found 'em.'

Aunt Augusta gave a little gasp of terror.

William's heart was less stony than he liked to think. Her terror touched him and he relented.

'Look here,' he said, 'I think p'raps that path'll get us out. Let's try that path.'

'No,' she panted. 'I'm simply exhausted. I can't walk another step just now. Besides it might only take us further into the heart of the wood.'

'Well, I'll go,' said William. 'I'll go an' see if it leads to the road.'

'No, you *certainly* mustn't,' said Aunt Augusta sharply, 'we must at all costs keep together. You'll miss your way and we shall both be lost separately. I've read of that happening in books. People lost in forests and one going on to find the way and losing the others. No, I'm certainly not going to risk that. I *forbid* you going a yard without me, William, and I'm too much exhausted to walk any more just at present.'

William, who had by now tired of the adventure and was anxious to draw it to an end as soon as possible, hesitated, then said vaguely:

'Well . . . s'pose I leave some sort of trail same as they do in books.'

'But what can you leave a trail of?' said Aunt Augusta.

Suddenly William's face shone as if illuminated by a light within. He only just prevented himself from turning a somersault into the middle of a blackberry bush.

'I've got an envelope in my pocket,' he said. 'I'll tear that up. I mean—' he added cryptically, 'it's a case of life and death, isn't it?'

'Do be careful then, dear boy,' said Aunt Augusta anxiously. 'Drop it every *inch* of the way. I hope it's something you can spare, by the way?'

'Oh yes,' William assured her, 'it's something I can spare all right.'

He took the report out of his pocket, and began to tear it into tiny fragments. He walked slowly down the path, dropping the pieces, and taking the precaution of tearing each piece into further fragments as he dropped it. There must be no possibility of its being rescued and put together again. Certain sentences, for instance the one that said, 'Uniformly bad. Has made no progress at all,' he tore up till the paper on which they were written was almost reduced to its component elements.

The path led, as William had known it would, round a corner and immediately into the main road. He returned a few minutes later, having assumed an expression of intense surprise and delight.

'S'all right,' he announced, 'the road's jus' round there.'

Aunt Augusta took out a handkerchief and mopped her brow.

'I'm so glad, dear boy,' she said. 'So very glad. What a relief! I was just wondering how one told edible from inedible berries. We might, as you said, have been here for days . . . Now let's just sit here and rest a few minutes before we go home. Is it far by the road?'

'No,' said William. 'There's a 'bus that goes all the way.'

'S'POSE I LEAVE A TRAIL,' SAID WILLIAM, 'SAME AS THEY DO IN BOOKS?'

He took his seat by her on the log, trying to restrain the exuberant expansiveness of his grin. His fingers danced a dance of triumph in his empty pockets.

'I was so much relieved, dear boy,' went on Aunt Augusta, 'to see you coming back again. It would have been so terrible if we'd lost each other. By the way, what was the paper that you tore up, dear? Nothing important, I hope?'

William had his face well under control by now.

'It was my school report,' he said, 'I was jus' takin' it home when I met you.'

He spoke sorrowfully as one who has lost his dearest treasure.

Aunt Augusta's face registered blank horror.

'You—you tore up your school report?' she said faintly.

'I had to,' said William. 'I'd rather,' he went on, assuming an expression of noble self-sacrifice, 'I'd rather, lose my school report than have you starve to death.'

It was clear that, though Aunt Augusta was deeply touched by this, her horror still remained.

'But—your school report, dear boy,' she said. 'It's dreadful to think of your sacrificing that for me. I remember so well the joy and pride of the moment when I handed my school report to my parents. I'm sure you know that moment well.'

William, not knowing what else to do, heaved a deep sigh.

'Was it,' said Aunt Augusta, still in a tone of deep concern and sympathy, 'was it a *specially* good one?'

'We aren't allowed to look at them,' said William unctuously; 'they always tell us to take them straight home to our parents without looking at them.'

'Of course. Of course,' said Aunt Augusta. 'Quite right, of course, but—oh, how disappointing for you, dear boy. You have some idea no doubt what sort of a report it was?'

'Oh yes,' said William, 'I've got some sort of an idea all right.'

'And I'm sure, dear,' said Aunt Augusta, 'that it was a very, very good one.'

William's expression of complacent modesty was rather convincing.

'Well . . . I—I dunno,' he said self-consciously.

'I'm sure it was,' said Aunt Augusta. 'I know it was. And *you* know it was really. I can tell that, dear boy, from the way you speak of it.'

'Oh . . . I dunno,' said William, intensifying the expression of complacent modesty that was being so successful. 'I dunno . . .'

'And that tells me that it was,' said Aunt Augusta triumphantly, 'far more plainly than if you said it was. I like a boy to be modest about his attainments. I don't like a boy to go about boasting of his successes in school. I'm sure you never do that, do you, dear boy?'

'Oh no,' said William with perfect truth. 'No, I never do that.'

'But I'm so worried about the loss of your report. How quietly and calmly you sacrificed it.' It was clear that her appreciation of William's nobility was growing each minute. 'Couldn't we try to pick up the bits on our way to the road and piece them together for your dear father to see?'

'Yes,' said William. 'Yes, we could try'n' do that.'

He spoke brightly, happy in the consciousness that he had torn up the paper into such small pieces that it couldn't possibly be put together.

'Let's start now, dear, shall we?' said Aunt Augusta; 'I'm quite rested.'

They went slowly along the little path that led to the road.

Aunt Augusta picked up the 'oo' of 'poor' and said, 'This must be a "good" of course,' and she picked up the 'ex' of 'extremely lazy and inattentive' and said, 'This must be an "excellent" of course,' but even Aunt Augusta realised that it would be impossible to put together all the pieces.

'I'm afraid it can't be done, dear,' she said sadly. 'How

*disappointing* for you. I feel so sorry that I mentioned it at all. It must have raised your hopes.'

'No, it's quite all right,' said William, 'it's quite all right. I'm not disappointed. Really I'm not.'

'I *know* what you're feeling, dear boy,' said Aunt Augusta. 'I know what I should feel myself in your place. And I hope—I *hope* that I'd have been as brave about it as you are.'

William, not knowing what to say, sighed again. He was beginning to find his sigh rather useful. They had reached the road now. A 'bus was already in sight. Aunt Augusta hailed it, and they boarded it together. They completed the journey to William's house in silence. Once Aunt Augusta gave William's hand a quick surreptitious pressure of sympathy and whispered:

'I know *just* what you are feeling, dear boy.'

William, hoping that she didn't, hastily composed his features to their expression of complacent modesty, tinged with deep disappointment—the expression of a boy who has had the misfortune to lose a magnificent school report.

His father was at home, and came to the front door to greet Aunt Augusta.

'Hello!' he said. 'Picked up William on the way?'

He spoke without enthusiasm. He wasn't a mercenary man, but this was his only rich unmarried aunt, and he'd

'WE WERE COMPLETELY LOST, RIGHT IN THE HEART OF THE WOOD,' SAID AUNT AUGUSTA. 'BUT THIS DEAR BOY WENT ON TO EXPLORE.'

hoped that she wouldn't see too much of William on her visit.

Aunt Augusta at once began to pour out a long and confused account of her adventure.

'And we were *completely* lost . . . right in the heart of the wood. I was too much exhausted to go a step farther,

WILLIAM GAZED INTO THE DISTANCE AS IF HE SAW NEITHER HIS FATHER NOR AUNT AUGUSTA.

but this dear boy went on to explore and, solely on my account because I was nervous of our being separated, he tore up his school report to mark the trail. It was, of course, a great sacrifice for the dear boy, because he was looking forward with such pride and pleasure to watching you read it.'

William gazed into the distance as if he saw neither his father nor Aunt Augusta. Only so could he retain his expression of patient suffering.

'Oh, he was, was he?' said Mr. Brown sardonically, but in the presence of his aunt forbore to say more.

During lunch, Aunt Augusta, who had completely forgotten her exhaustion and was beginning to enjoy the sensation of having been lost in a wood, enlarged upon the subject of William and the lost report.

'Without a word and solely in order to allay my anxiety, he gave up what I know to be one of the proudest moments one's schooldays have to offer. I'm not one of those people who forget what it is to be a child. I can see myself now handing my report to my mother and father and watching their faces radiant with pride and pleasure as they read it. I'm sure that is a sight that you have often seen, dear boy?'

William, who was finding his expression of virtue hard to sustain under his father's gaze, took refuge in a prolonged fit of coughing which concentrated Aunt Augusta's attention upon him all the more.

'I *do* hope he hasn't caught a cold in that nasty damp wood,' she said anxiously. 'He took *such* care of me, and I shall never forget the sacrifice he made for me.'

'*Was* it a good report, William?' said Mrs. Brown with tactless incredulity.

William turned to her an expressionless face.

'We aren't allowed to look at 'em,' he said virtuously. 'He tells us to bring 'em home without lookin' at 'em.'

'But I could tell it was a good report,' said Aunt Augusta. 'He wouldn't admit it but I could *tell* that he *knew* it was a good report. He bore it very bravely but I saw what a grief it was to him to have to destroy it—' Suddenly her face beamed. 'I know, I've got an idea! Couldn't you write to the headmaster and ask for a duplicate?'

William's face was a classic mark of horror.

'No, don't do that,' he pleaded, 'don't do that. I-I-I,' with a burst of inspiration, 'I shun't like to give 'em so much trouble in the holidays.'

Aunt Augusta put her hand caressingly on his stubbly head. '*Dear* boy,' she said.

William escaped after lunch, but, before he joined the Outlaws, he went to the wood and ground firmly into the mud with his heel whatever traces of the torn report could be seen.

It was tea time when he returned. Aunt Augusta had departed. His father was reading a book by the fire. William hovered about uneasily for some minutes.

Then Mr. Brown, without raising his eyes from his book, said, 'Funny thing, you getting lost in Croome Wood, William. I should have thought you knew every inch of it. Never been lost in it before, have you?'

'No,' said William, and then after a short silence:

'I say . . . father.'

'Yes,' said Mr. Brown.

'Are you—are you really goin' to write for another report?'

'What sort of a report actually *was* the one you lost?' said Mr. Brown, fixing him with a gimlet eye, 'Was it a very bad one?'

William bore the gimlet eye rather well.

'We aren't allowed to look at 'em, you know,' he said again innocently. 'I told you we're told to bring 'em straight home without looking at 'em.'

Mr. Brown was silent for a minute. As I said before, he wasn't a mercenary man, but he couldn't help being glad of the miraculously good impression that William had made on his only rich unmarried aunt.

'I don't believe,' he said slowly, 'that there's the slightest atom of doubt, but I'll give you the benefit of it all the same.'

William leapt exultantly down the garden and across the fields to meet the Outlaws.

They heard him singing a quarter of a mile away.

CHAPTER 3

# THE CHRISTMAS TRUCE

It was Hubert's mother's idea that the Outlaws versus Hubert Laneites feud should be abolished.

'Christmas, you know,' she said vaguely to William's mother, 'the season of peace and goodwill. If they don't bury the hatchet at this season they never will. It's so absurd for them to go on like this. Think how much *happier* they'd be if they were *friends*.'

Mrs. Brown thought, murmured 'Er—yes,' uncertainly, and added, 'I've *tried,* you know, but boys are so funny.'

'Yes,' said Mrs. Lane earnestly (Mrs. Lane was large and breathless and earnest and overdressed), 'but they're *very* sweet, aren't they? Hubie's *awfully* sweet. I simply can't think how anyone could quarrel with Hubie. We'll make a *real* effort this Christmas to put an end to this foolish quarrel, won't we? I feel that if only your Willie got to know my Hubie properly, he'd simply love him, he would really. *Everyone* who really knows Hubie loves him.'

Mrs. Brown said, 'Er—yes,' still more uncertainly, and

Mrs. Lane continued: 'I've thought out how to do it. If you'll invite Hubie to Willie's party, we'll *insist* on his coming, and we'll invite Willie to Hubie's, and you *insist* on his coming, and then it will be all right. They'll have got to know each other, and, I'm sure, learnt to love each other.'

Mrs. Brown said 'Er—yes,' more uncertainly than ever. She felt that Mrs. Lane was being unduly optimistic, but still it *would* be nice to see the end of the feud that was always leading William into such wild and desperate adventures.

'Then we'll begin by—'

'Begin and end, my dear Mrs. Brown,' said Mrs. Lane earnestly, 'by making them attend each other's Christmas parties. I'm absolutely convinced that they'll *love* each other after that. I know anyway that Willie will love Hubie, because, when you really get to know Hubie, he's the most *lovable* boy you can possibly imagine.'

Mrs. Brown said 'Er—yes,' again, because she couldn't think of anything else to say, and so the matter was settled.

When it was broached to William, he was speechless with horror.

'*Him?*' he exploded fiercely when at last the power of speech returned to him. 'Ask *him* to my Christmas party? I'd sooner not have a Christmas party at all than ask *him* to it. *Him!* Why I wun't go to the *King's* Christmas party, if *he* was going to be there. Not if I had to be beheaded for it. *Him?* Well, then I jolly well won't have a party at all.'

But Mrs. Brown was unexpectedly firm. The overtures, she said, had come from Hubert's mother, and they could not with decency be rejected. It was the season of peace and goodwill ('No one's ever peaceful or goodwillin' to me at it,' put in William bitterly); and we must all bury the hatchet and start afresh.

'I don't want to bury no hatchet,' said William tempestuously, ' 'cept in his head. *Him!* Wantin' to come to my party! *Cheek!*'

But William's tempestuous fury was as usual of no avail against his mother's gentle firmness.

'It's no use, William,' she said. 'I've *promised.* He's to come to your party, and you're to go to his, and Mrs. Lane is quite sure that you'll be real friends after it.'

'*Me* friends with *him!*' exploded William. 'I'll never be friends with him 'cept in a lunatic asylum an'—'

'But William,' said his mother, stemming his flood of frenzied oratory, 'I'm sure he's a very nice little boy when you get to know him.'

William replied to this by a (partially) dumb and very realistic show of physical nausea.

But faced by the alternative of Hubert Lane and his friends as guests at his party or no party at all, William bowed to the inevitable.

'All right,' he said, 'I'll have him then an'—all right, I won't *do* anythin' to him or to any of them I'll wait till it's all over. I'll wait till he's been to my party an' I've been to his, an' then—well, you'll be jolly sorry you ever made us do it 'cause we'll have such a lot to make up.'

Mrs. Brown, however, was content with her immediate victory. She sent an invitation to Hubert Lane and to Bertie Franks (Hubert's friend and lieutenant) and to Hubert's other friends, and they all accepted in their best copper-plate handwriting. William and his Outlaws went about sunk deep in gloom.

'If it wasn't for the trifle an' the crackers,' said William darkly, 'I wouldn't have had it at all—not with *him*. An' it'll have to be a jolly fine trifle, practic'ly *all* cream, to make it worth while.' His mood grew darker and darker as the day approached. He even discussed with his Outlaws the possibility of making a raid on the larder before the party, and carrying off trifles and jellies and fruit salad into the woods, leaving the Hubert Laneites to arrive and find the cupboard bare and their hosts flown. It was a tempting plan, but after dallying with it fondly for a few days they reluctantly gave it up, as being not really worth its inevitable consequences. Instead, they steeled themselves to go through the affair in the dogged spirit of martyrdom, their sufferings allayed only by the thought of the trifle and crackers, and the riot of hositilities that could take place as soon as the enforced Christmas truce was over. For the prospect of the end of the feud brought no glow of joy to the Outlaws' hearts. Without the Hubert Lane feud life would be dull indeed.

As the day of the party drew nearer, curiosity lightened the gloom of their spirits. How would the Hubert Laneites behave? Would they come reluctantly, surlily, at the bidding of authority, or would they come in a Christmas spirit of peace and goodwill, genuinely anxious to bury the hatchet? The latter possibility was too horrible to contemplate. Rather let them come in the spirit in which the Outlaws were prepared to receive them—a spirit in which one receives a deadly foe in time of truce, all their thoughts and energies centred on the happy moment when hostilities might be resumed.

William, of course, could not watch the preparations for his party and maintain unbroken his pose of aloof displeasure. The trifle was, he was convinced, the finest trifle that had yet been seen in the neighbourhood; there were jellies of every shape and hue, there was a cream blancmange decorated with cherries and angelica, and there was an enormous iced Christmas cake. *And* there were crackers. In the eyes of William and his friends it was the crackers that lent the final touch of festivity to the tea.

The Outlaws and their supporters, as arranged, arrived first, and stood round William like a body-guard awaiting the arrival of the Hubert Laneites. They wore perfectly blank expressions, prepared to meet the Hubert Laneites in whatever guise they presented themselves. And the guise in which they ultimately presented themselves was worse than the Outlaws' worst fears. They were not surly foes, forced reluctantly to simulate neutrality, nor were they heralds of peace and goodwill. They advanced upon their host with an oily friendliness that was nauseating. They winked at each other openly. They said, 'Thanks *so* much for asking us, William. It was ripping of you. Oh, I say . . . what *topping* decorations!'

And they nudged each other and sniggered. William clenched his fists in his coat pocket and did swift mental calculations. His party would be over in four hours. In four days' time Hubert's party would come, and that would last about four hours, and then, *then*, THEN they could jolly well look out for themselves. The right hand that was clenched tightly in his coat for safety's sake was itching to plant itself firmly in Hubert's smug and smiling face. Mrs. Brown, of course, was deceived by their show of friendliness.

'There, William,' she whispered triumphantly, 'I knew it would be all right. They're so nice really, and *so* grateful to you for asking them. I'm sure you'll be the *greatest* friends after this. His mother *said* that he was a nice little boy.'

William did not reply to this because there wasn't anything that he could trust himself to say. He was still restraining himself with great difficulty from hurling himself upon his foes. They went in to tea.

'Oh, I saw how *ripping!* How *topping!*' said the Hubert Laneites gushingly to Mrs. Brown, nudging each other and sniggering whenever her eye was turned away from them. Once Hubert looked at William and made his most challenging grimace, turning immediately to Mrs. Brown to say with an ingratiating smile:

'It's a simply topping party, Mrs. Brown, and it's awfully nice of you to ask us.'

Mrs. Brown beamed at him and said:

'It's so nice to *have* you, Hubert,' and the other Hubert Laneites sniggered, and William kept his hands in his pockets with such violence that one of them went right through the lining. But the crowning catastrophe happened when they pulled the crackers.

Hubert went up to William, and said, 'See what I've got out of a cracker, William,' and held up a ring that sent a squirt of water into William's face. The Hubert Laneites went into paroxysms of silent laughter. Hubert was all smirking contrition.

'I say, I'm so sorry, William, I'd no idea that it would do that. I'm frightfully sorry, Mrs. Brown. I'd no idea that it would do that. I just got it out of one of the crackers. I say, I'm *so* sorry, William.'

It was evident to everyone but Mrs. Brown that the ring had not come out of a cracker, but had been carefully brought by Hubert in order to play this trick on William. William was wiping water out of his eyes and ears.

'It's quite all right, dear,' said Mrs. Brown. 'It was *quite* an accident, we all saw. They shouldn't have such nasty things in crackers, but it wasn't your fault. Tell him that you don't mind a bit, William.'

But William hastily left the room.

'Now let's go and have a few games, shall we?' said Mrs. Brown.

Ginger followed William upstairs, and found him on the hearthrug in his bedroom, kneeling over a bolster that he was violently pummelling. Ginger knew that to William the bolster was not the bolster, but Hubert Lane's plump, well-nourished body. William raised a shining purple face from his task, and then the glow faded from it as he realised that the prostrate form before him was merely the bolster, and that Hubert Lane was triumphantly sniggering among his friends downstairs, not yet overtaken by Nemesis.

'Why don't you go down and smash his face in?' said Ginger simply.

William, returning reluctantly to Reality, raised the limp form of the bolster, and threw it on to the bed.

'Can't,' he said tersely, 'can't do anything not while he's in our house. I—'

'William, darling,' called his mother, 'Come down, we're going to begin the games.'

William and Ginger went downstairs, and the rest of the party passed off uneventfully. The Hubert Laneites said good-bye at the end with nauseous gratitude, and went sniggering down the drive.

'*There,* William!' said Mrs. Brown, as she shut the door, 'I knew it would be all right. They were so grateful and they enjoyed it *so* much and you're *quite* friends now, aren't you?'

But William was already upstairs in his bedroom, pummelling his bolster with such energy that he burst his collar open. During the days that intervened between William's party and Hubert Lane's party, the Hubert

Laneites kept carefully out of the way of the Outlaws. Yet the Outlaws felt uneasily that something was brewing. Not content with scoring over them at William's party, Hubert meant to score over them in some way at his own. The Hubert Laneites looked upon the truce, not as something that tied their hands for the time being, but as something that delivered their enemies into their power. William was uneasily aware that Hubert Lane would not feel the compunction that he had felt in the matter of his guests.

'We've gotter do somethin' to them at their party, same as they did to us at ours,' said Ginger firmly.

'Yes, but what can we do?' said William. 'We can't start fightin' 'em. We've promised not to. An'—an' there's nothin' else we *can* do. Jus' wait, jus' *wait* till their party's over.'

And William's fists curled themselves zestfully as he danced his most fiendish war dance in the middle of the road (his bolster had been so badly used lately that nearly all the feathers were coming out. Mrs. Brown had asked him only that morning what on earth he was doing to it).

'But they'll never forget that water squirt,' said Ginger mournfully.

'Unless we do somethin' back,' said Douglas.

'What *can* we do in *their* house with them watchin'

us all the time?' said Henry.

'We mus' jus' *think*,' said William, 'there's four days an' we'll think hard.'

But the day of Hubert's party arrived, and they'd thought of nothing. William looked downcast and spiritless. Even pummelling his bolster had lost its charm for him.

They met in the old barn in the morning to arrange their plan of action, but none of them could think of any plan of action to arrange, and the meeting broke up gloomily at lunch time, without having come to any decision at all.

William walked slowly and draggingly through the village on his way home. His mother had told him to stop at the baker's with an order for her, and it was a sign of his intense depression that he remembered to do it. In ordinary circumstances William forgot his mother's messages in the village. He entered the baker's shop, and stared around him resentfully. It seemed to be full of people. He'd have to wait all night before anyone took any notice of him. Just his luck, he reflected bitterly . . . Then he suddenly realised that the mountainous lady just in front of him was Mrs. Lane. She was talking in a loud voice to a friend.

'Yes, Hubie's party is this afternoon. We're having William Brown and his friends. To put a stop to that silly quarrel that's gone on so long, you know. Hubie's so lovable that I simply can't think how anyone could quarrel with him. But, of course, it will be all right after to-day. We've having a Father Christmas, you know. Bates, our gardener, is going to be the Father Christmas and give out presents. I've given Hubie three pounds to get some *really* nice presents for it to celebrate the ending of the feud.'

William waited his turn, gave his message, and went home for lunch.

Immediately after lunch he made his way to Bates's cottage.

It stood on the road at the end of the Lanes' garden. One gate led from the garden to the road, and the other from the garden to the Lanes' shrubbery. Behind the cottage was Bates's treasured kitchen garden, and at the bottom was a little shed where he stored his apples. The window of the shed had to be open for airing purposes, but Bates kept a sharp look out for his perpetual and inveterate enemies, boys.

William approached the cottage with great circumspection, looking anxiously around to be sure that none of the Hubert Laneites was in sight. He had reckoned on the likelihood of their all being engaged in preparation for the party.

He opened the gate, walked up the path, and knocked at the door, standing poised on one foot ready to turn to flee should Bates, recognising him and remembering some of his former exploits in his kitchen garden, attack him on sight. He heaved a sigh of relief, however, when Bates opened the door. It was clear that Bates did not recognise him. He received him with an ungracious scowl, but that, William could see, was because he was *a* boy, not because he was *the* boy.

'Well?' said Bates sharply, holding the door open a few inches, 'what d'you want?'

William assumed an ingratiating smile, the smile of a boy who has every right to demand admittance to the cottage.

'I say,' he said with a fairly good imitation of the Hubert Laneites' most patronising manner, 'you've got the Father Christmas things here, haven't you?'

The ungraciousness of Bates's scowl did not relax, but he opened the door a few inches wider in a resigned fashion. He had been pestered to death over the Father Christmas things. These boys had been in and out of his cottage all day with parcels and what not, trampling over his doorstep and 'mussing up' everything. He'd decided some time ago that it wasn't going to be worth the five shillings that Mrs. Lane was giving him for it. He took for granted that William was one of the Hubert Laneites coming once more to 'muss up' his bag of parcels, and take one out or put one in, or snigger over them as they'd been doing every day for the last week. But he *did* think that they'd have left him in peace on the very afternoon of the party.

'Yes,' he said surlily, 'I've got the things 'ere an' they're all right, so there's no call to start upsettin' of 'em again. I've had enough of you comin' in an' mussin' the place up.'

'I only wanted to count them, and make sure that we've got the right number,' said William with an oily friendliness that was worthy of Hubert himself.

The man opened the door with a shrug.

'All right,' he said, 'go in and count 'em. I tell you, I'm sick of the whole lot of you, I am. Mussin' the place up. Look at your boots!'

William looked at his boots, made an ineffectual attempt to wipe them on the mat, and entered the cottage. He had an exhilarating sense of danger and adventure as he entered. At any minute he might arouse the man's suspicions. His ignorance of where the presents were, for instance, when he was supposed to have been visiting them regularly, might give him away completely. Moreover, a Hubert Laneite might arrive any minute and trap him, in the cottage. It was, in short, a situation after William's own heart. The immediate danger of discovery was averted by Bates himself, who waved him irascibly into the back parlour, where the presents were evidently kept. William entered, and threw a quick glance out of the window. Yes, Ginger was there, as they had arranged he should be, hovering near the shed where the apples were sorted. Then he looked round the room. A red cloak and hood and white beard were spread out on the sofa, and on the hearthrug lay a sackful of small parcels.

'Well, count 'em for goodness' sake an' let's get a bit of peace,' said Bates more irritably than ever. William fell on his knees and began to make a pretence of counting the parcels. Suddenly he looked up and gazed out of the window.

'I say!' he said, 'there's a boy taking your apples.'

Bates leapt to the window. There, upon the roof of the shed, was Ginger, with an arm through the open window, obviously in the act of purloining apples and carefully exposing himself to view.

With a yell of fury Bates sprang to the door and down the path towards the shed. He had forgotten everything but this outrage upon his property. Left alone, William turned his attention quickly to the sack. It contained parcels, each one labelled and named. He had to act quickly. Bates had set off after Ginger, but he might return at any minute. Ginger's instructions were to lure him on by keeping just out of reach, but Bates might tire of the chase before they'd gone a few yards, and, remembering his visitor, return to the cottage in order to prevent his 'mussin'' things up any more than necessary. William had no time to investigate. He had to act solely upon his suspicions and his knowledge of the characters of Hubert and his friends. Quickly he began to change the labels of the little parcels, putting the one marked William on to the one marked Hubert, and exchanging the labels of the Outlaws and their supporters for those of the Hubert Laneites and their supporters. Just as he was fastening the last one, Bates returned, hot and breathless.

'Did you catch him?' said William, secure in the knowledge that Ginger had outstripped Bates more times than any of them could remember.

'Naw,' said Mr. Bates, panting and furious. 'I'd like to wring his neck. I'd larn him if I got hold of him. Who was he? Did you see?'

'He was about the same size as me,' said William in the bright, eager tone of one who is trying to help, 'or he may have been just a *tiny* bit smaller.'

Bates turned upon him, as if glad of the chance to vent

his irascibility upon somebody.

'Well, you clear out,' he said, 'I've had enough of you mussin' the place up, an' you can tell the others that they can keep away too. An' I'll be glad when it's over, I tell you. I'm sick of the lot of you.'

Smiling the patronising smile that he associated with the Hubert Laneites, William took a hurried departure, and ran home as quickly as he could. He found his mother searching for him despairingly.

'Oh, William, where *have* you been? You ought to have begun to get ready for the party *hours* ago.'

'I've just been for a little walk,' said William casually. 'I'll be ready in time all right.'

With the unwelcome aid of his mother, he was ready in time, spick and span and spruce and shining.

'I'm so *glad* that you're friends now and that that silly quarrel's over,' said Mrs. Brown as she saw him off. 'You feel much *happier* now that you're friends, don't you?'

William snorted sardonically, and set off down the road.

The Hubert Laneites received the Outlaws with even more nauseous friendliness than they had shown at William's house. It was evident, however, from the way they sniggered and nudged each other that they had some plan prepared. William felt anxious. Suppose that the plot they had so obviously prepared had nothing to do with the Father Christmas . . . Suppose that he had wasted his time and trouble that morning . . . They went into the hall after tea, and Mrs. Lane said roguishly:

'Now, boys, I've got a visitor for you.' Immediately Bates, inadequately disguised as Father Christmas and looking fiercely resentful of the whole proceedings, entered with his sack. The Hubert Laneites sniggered delightedly. This was evidently the crowning moment of the afternoon. Bates took the parcels out one by one, announcing the name on each label.

The first was William.

The Hubert Laneites watched him go up to receive it in paroxysms of silent mirth. William took it and opening it, wearing a sphinx-like expression. It was the most magnificent mouth organ that he had ever seen. The mouths of the Hubert Laneites dropped open in horror and amazement. It was evidently the present that Hubert had destined for himself. Bates called out Hubert's name. Hubert, his mouth still hanging open with horror and amazement, went to receive his parcel. It contained a short pencil with shield and rubber of the sort that can be purchased for a penny or twopence. He went back to his seat blinking. He examined his label. It bore his name. He examined William's label. It bore his name. There was

BATES CALLED OUT THE NAMES ONE BY ONE.
THE FIRST WAS WILLIAM.

IT WAS THE MOST MAGNIFICENT MOUTH ORGAN THAT HE HAD EVER SEEN. THE HUBERT LANEITES STARED IN HORROR AND AMAZEMENT.

no mistake about it. William was thanking Mrs. Lane effusively for his present.

'Yes, dear,' she was saying, 'I'm so glad you like it. I haven't had time to look at them but I told Hubie to get nice things.'

Hubert opened his mouth to protest, and then shut it again. He was beaten and he knew it. He couldn't very well tell his mother that he'd spent the bulk of the money on the presents for himself and his particular friends, and had spent only a few coppers on the Outlaws' presents. He couldn't think what had happened. He'd been so sure that it would be all right. The Outlaws would hardly have had the nerve publicly to object to their presents, and Mrs. Lane was well meaning but conveniently short sighted, and took for granted that everything that Hubie did was perfect. Hubert sat staring at his pencil and blinking his eyes in incredulous horror. Meanwhile the presentation was going on. Bertie Franks' present was a ruler that could not have cost more than a penny, and Ginger's was a magnificent electric torch. Bertie stared at the torch with an expression that would have done credit to a tragic mask, and Ginger hastened to establish his permanent right to his prize by going up to thank Mrs. Lane for it.

'Yes, it's lovely, dear,' she said, 'I told Hubie to get nice things.'

Douglas's present was a splendid penknife, and Henry's a fountain-pen, while the corresponding presents for the Hubert Laneites were an indiarubber and a note-book. The Hubert Laneites watched their presents passing into the enemies' hands with expressions of helpless agony. But Douglas's parcel had more than a penknife in it. It had a little bunch of imitation flowers with an india-rubber bulb attached and a tiny label, 'Show this to William and press the rubber thing.' Douglas took it to Hubert. Hubert knew it, of course, for he had bought it, but he was paralysed with horror at the whole situation.

'Look, Hubert,' said Douglas.

A fountain of ink caught Hubert neatly in the eye. Douglas was all surprise and contrition.

'I'm so sorry, Hubert,' he said, 'I'd no idea that it was going to do that. I've just got it out of my parcel and I'd no idea that it was going to do that. I'm so sorry, Mrs. Lane. I'd no idea that it was going to do that.'

'Of course you hadn't, dear,' said Mrs. Lane. 'It's Hubies's own fault for buying a thing like that. It's very foolish of him indeed.'

Hubert wiped the ink out of his eyes and sputtered helplessly.

Then William discovered that it was time to go.

'Thank you so much for our lovely presents, Hubert,'

he said politely, 'we've had a *lovely* time.'

And Hubert, under his mother's eye, smiled a green and sickly smile.

The Outlaws marched triumphantly down the road, brandishing their spoils. William was playing on his mouth organ, Ginger was flashing his electric light, Henry waving his fountain-pen, and Douglas slashing at the hedge with his penknife.

Occasionally they turned round to see if their enemies were pursuing them, in order to retrieve their treasures.

But the Hubert Laneites were too broken in spirit to enter into open hostilities just then.

As they walked, the Outlaws raised a wild and inharmonious pæan of triumph.

And over the telephone Mrs. Lane was saying to Mrs. Brown:

'Yes, dear, it's been a *complete* success. They're the *greatest* friends now. I'm sure it's been a Christmas that they'll all remember all their lives.'

CHAPTER 4

# WILLIAM HELPS THE CAUSE

When first William and his friends heard of the Grand Bazaar that was to be held in the grounds of the Hall in aid of the Church Schools of the district, they were wholly unmoved.

They didn't take any interest in bazaars, they didn't take any interest in the grounds of the Hall, which were very prim and uninteresting, and they didn't take any interest in the Church Schools of the district.

The present tenants of the Hall were an ultra correct couple of unimpeachable aristocracy, who treated the village and its inhabitants as if they didn't exist. William and his friends did not resent this. It was, they considered, preferable to the attitude of some other of their neighbours, but it made the Veritys negligible as human beings. They were not the kind of people who would join in fun, or the kind of people who objected to fun. Out of both these kinds the Outlaws could be counted on to extract entertainment. The Veritys merely ignored fun. Sir George Verity was reputed to have one of the finest collections of miniatures in England, and Lady Verity the most paralysing way with a pair of lorgnettes.

Her name figured in lists of guests at important functions. Her photograph appeared in the papers in elegant but languid poses, looking as if she hadn't really wanted to be taken, and wished they'd hurry up and get it over.

The village was vaguely proud of them, though slightly piqued at being so completely ignored by them. It loved to read of his miniatures and her dresses, but it didn't like being stared at distantly from the haughty fastness of a Rolls Royce.

Had the bazaar for the Church Schools been a purely local effort, the Veritys would have lent it neither their countenance nor their grounds. But it wasn't. The other parishes for miles around were joining in it, and the Bishop was coming to it, therefore the Veritys offered their grounds, their countenances, and their names at the head of the subscription list.

The first meeting was to be held at the Hall, and an invitation had been sent to most of the local people, including William's mother, to attend. Mrs. Brown was mildly interested.

'I don't mind what I do,' she confided to her family. 'Only I do hope they don't put me on the rummage stall. It's so wearing.'

'I'd try'n' get on the refreshment stall if I were you,' William advised her, 'that's the stall I'd always try'n' get on if I helped at bazaars an' things. Not that I'd ever get on anythin' I wanted to,' he added bitterly. 'I never have any luck.'

William was recovering from 'flu, and was not feeling his brightest and best. The doctor had said that he was not to go back to school till next week, and Mrs. Brown was finding the days almost as long as did William himself. For all William's friends were at school, and William alone, bored and irritable, with no outlets for his energy (which seemed quite unimpaired by his illness), was not the most restful of companions.

They gave him books to read, but William unfortunately was not a reader. Instead he experimented with the hot water system, trying to 'lay on' water from the bathroom to his bedroom in rubber tubes and being surprised and aggrieved by the resultant floods.

'Well, I didn't know it was goin' to do that. It mus' be somethin' wrong with the way the pipes are made in this house. Well, it ought to've jus' flowed through the tube an' not made a mess at all. Well, I can't help it. I've gotter do *somethin'*, haven't I?'

On the morning of the bazaar meeting at the Hall he had tried to make an electric train out of a small electric battery and the cook's favourite cake tin, in which he had bored holes in order to affix wheels taken from an old toy engine. The cook had swooped down on him in fury in the middle, and, flinging herself incautiously upon the 'train', had received an electric shock. Though not seriously hurt, she had screamed continuously for a quarter of an hour, and it had taken all Mrs. Brown's tact to calm her.

'Well, all I can say, 'm',' she said after saying a good deal more, 'is that if I'm to be left in the same house with that there limb this afternoon I hands in me notice here and now.'

She was a good cook, so Mrs. Brown hastened to assure her that she wouldn't be left alone in the house with that there limb, and then turned to consider the situation. She might, of course, stay at home, but she did want to attend the meeting at the Hall. She asked William if he'd like to go for a good long walk that afternoon, and he replied without any hesistation that he wouldn't.

Then she glanced at her invitation. It plainly said: 'Please bring anyone else who may be interested.'

'William,' she said firmly, 'you must come with me to the meeting this afternoon.'

'*Me?*' said William indignantly. '*Me?* D'you mean *me*?'

'Of course I mean you,' said Mrs. Brown wearily, 'I can't leave you here. You won't go for a walk and so you must come with me.'

William, changing his tactics, adopted the air of a suffering invalid.

'I'm not strong enough,' he said in a faint voice, 'I've only jus' finished bein' ill. Seems to me you want to *kill* me takin' me out to meetin's when I ought to be restin' at home.'

'Well, if you'll go to bed and rest, you can stay here,' said his mother.

'It's not *that* sort of restin' I mean,' said William hastily, 'I mean jus' goin' gently about an'—an', well, jus' goin' gently about.'

'As you did this morning?'

'Yes,' said William unguardedly.

'That settles it,' said his mother. 'You must come with me. I don't want to lose cook. We've never had anyone else who got the Yorkshire pudding just as your father likes it.'

'You don't mind losin' me,' muttered William fiercely, 'riskin' my life draggin' me out to meetin's when I ought to be stayin' gently at home gettin' up my strength to go back to school. *That's* why I don't want to go to the meetin', because I want to get strong again to go back to school. I don't want to get behind in my work.'

But it was useless, and William knew that it was useless. His mother was determined. So he surrendered himself in a spirit of gloomy pessimism to be washed and brushed till he shone again, and arrayed in his hated best suit. He had an inspiration in the middle, and said that he was feeling very ill, but on being offered a dose of his medicine said that he felt quite well again.

'Though if I *do* die of it,' he said bitterly—'and I shouldn't be surprised if I do, bein' dragged out to meetin's when I ought to be restin' quietly at home—I hope you won't be worried rememb'rin' that it was all your fault.'

His mother assured him that she wouldn't, and he relapsed into a gloomy silence.

He glared ferociously at the footman who opened the door of the Hall for them, at the butler who announced them, at Lady Verity, tall and elegant and miles and miles and miles away, who received them, and at all the other members of the meeting who sat around them. The Bishop was not there. There were several clergymen from the surrounding villages, a few local people, and—William. The meeting was as dull as such meetings generally are. Lady Verity wore an air of frigid aristocracy and suffering patience, as if she already regretted having involved herself in an affair that brought all these very ordinary people into her drawing-room.

'I've been speaking to the Bishop about it,' she said,

'and he suggests that, as the bazaar is for the Church Schools, one stall or entertainment should be undertaken by children. He thinks that it would be very nice.'

'Splendid idea,' said a breezy young clergyman from a village about seven miles off, who had only lately come there and hadn't heard of William. 'Simply splendid. It had better be the local children, of course. And not too many of them. How about'—his eyes wandered to William, whose expression of gloom gave him a misleading appearance of earnestness and virtue—'how about putting this young man in charge of it?'

There was a gasp from those who knew William, but the young man went on breezily:

'I take it that, as he's here, it means that he's interested in the scheme. I propose that we get him to collect one or two friends. and run one of the shows. Good policy to get the younger generation to help the cause.'

'I think that would be splendid,' said Lady Verity, whose one aim was to get the meeting over as quickly as possible. 'I'll tell the Bishop that's settled, then. And now what's the next thing to decide?'

Those who knew William had been so paralysed, and the thing had been arranged so quickly, that, by the time their power of speech returned to them, the discussion had left William far behind. In fact when Mrs. Brown at last found her voice and said, 'Oh, no, I think not. Really it wouldn't do at all,' the discussion had reached refreshments, and Lady Verity had just suggested that they should have tea on the terrace.

'But why wouldn't it do, Mrs. Brown?' said Lady Verity, raising her lorgnettes. 'The terrace seems to me an excellent place for tea.'

And Mrs. Brown realised that she had protested too late.

Though William preserved his blankest expression throughout the meeting, a close observer would have noticed that his gloom had lightened considerably.

The Vicar held a hasty consultation with Mrs. Brown immediately after the meeting. Relations between William and the Vicar were not cordial. The Vicar was a good man and an earnest worker, but he didn't understand even well-conducted boys, and he regarded William as one might regard a barrel of gunpowder that a spark will serve to ignite.

'I'm afraid it's too late to do anything,' he said. 'Unless you go back now and tell her that he's quite unsuited to be in charge of any side show.'

But Mrs. Brown objected to criticism of William from people outside the family, even the Vicar.

'Oh, I think he'll be all right,' she said rather coldly.

'He's really a very good worker when he gives his mind to anything.'

The Vicar, who had had frequent proofs of the result of William's work, hoped desperately that he wouldn't give his mind to this.

'You'd better not let him sell anything, anyway,' he said, remembering the time when William had inadvertently sold his wife's best coat, carelessly laid down for a moment upon the rummage stall.

'Oh, no,' said Mrs. Brown hastily, 'of course not. And, of course, I'll keep an eye on him.'

'I should think that it would be best for him to be in charge of some quiet competition.'

'Yes,' said Mrs. Brown, 'I'm *sure* that he'll do his best. I know that he sometimes makes mistakes, but he's really a very good boy.'

Mrs. Brown frequently made this statement, in the vague hope apparently that if she said it often enough it might become true.

'Er—yes,' said the Vicar in an unconvinced tone of voice.

'Well, we'll arrange details at our next meeting.'

William had not been listening to this conversation. He had been standing a short distance away, sunk deep in meditation. Though he still made spasmodic efforts to preserve his martyred expression, it was obvious that his meditations were not wholly unpleasant. When he saw that the conversation between his mother and the Vicar was over, he detached himself from his meditation, raised his cap with exaggerated politeness to the Vicar, and set off homeward with his mother.

'Well, you've been a very good boy, William,' said Mrs. Brown, who was relieved to have the afternoon safely over.

'For that show I'm goin' to have,' said William slowly, 'I think I'll get up a wild beast show.'

'*William!*' gasped Mrs. Brown. 'You mustn't *think* of such a thing.'

William looked at her in surprise.

'Why not?' he said. 'They said I could have a show, din't they? Well, they want to get money, don't they? Well, I bet people'll pay money to see a wild beast show, wun't they?'

'But William!' Mrs. Brown was still gasping with horror. 'You mustn't *think* of such a thing. You—you can't get any wild beasts for one thing, and even if you could—'

'Oh, can't I?' said William. 'I got up a jolly good wild beast show once and I could do it again too. Douglas's cat's jus' like a wild beast when you fasten it up an' one of Henry's white mice is a jolly good biter an' Jumble carries on jus' like a wild beast if you keep sayin' "rats" to him an' Ginger can act like a tiger so's you'd hardly know the diff'rence an'—'

'*No*, William. It's out of the question, so you mustn't *think* of it. They said "show," but they didn't mean a show of that sort. They meant a competition.'

'All right. I'll get up some wrestlin' matches. Anyone'd pay to see me and Ginger wrestlin'. I got all the buttons off his shirt the last time we had one. An' I tell you what I'll do. I'll challenge anyone in the audience to wrestle with me. I'll wear bathing drawers so's they can see my muscles an'—'

'*No*, William!' cried Mrs. Brown wildly.

'Well, then, a boxin' match. I'm a jolly good boxer an' I've made a jolly good pair of boxin' gloves out of an' old pair of gloves of father's, stuffin' 'em with paper. Las' time I had a boxin' match with Ginger, I made his nose bleed so's it went on bleedin' for nearly five minutes. Well, anyone'd pay to see that, wun't they? He made mine bleed, too, but it din't bleed as long as his. An' we'd challenge anyone in the audience to come an' box with us, an' I jolly well bet that—'

'*No*, William! They don't mean that sort of a competition.'

'What sort do they mean then?'

'Some sort of guessing competition.'

'All right. Ginger'n' me'll act wild animals an' they can guess which ones we're actin'.'

'*No*, William! They mean something quiet.'

'Well, we'll do it in dumb show an'—'

'*No*, William! You can't choose your own competition like that. You must wait and see what they tell you to do.'

'I bet it'll be somethin' jolly dull then,' said William gloomily.

He did not accompany Mrs. Brown to the next meeting, at which it was decided that William and his friends were to conduct a 'Butterfly Competition'.

The idea of the butterfly competition was that each competitor, upon payment of sixpence, should be given a piece of paper and be allowed three 'squeezes' from an assortment of paint tubes. This was then folded in the middle, and the effect that was judged to represent the best 'butterfly' won the prize.

William received the news of this with sardonic amusement. 'Well,' he said, 'if you think that people are goin' to like doin' that better than watchin' me an' Ginger wrestlin' an' boxin'—all I can say is that you've got a jolly funny idea of what people like.'

'If you don't think it's going to be interesting,' said Mrs. Brown with a gleam of hope, 'why not give it up and let someone else take it on?'

But it appeared that William was not prepared to do this.

'Oh no,' said William, 'I bet there's not many things that I can't make int'restin' even if they're not interestin' to start with.'

There was a sinister sound about this, but William, after his first outburst, seemed to be quite amenable. He promised to preside quietly over the tent, and to see that Douglas, Henry and Ginger, his helpers, were quiet too. He promised not to make a speech.

'You're there just to hand people's papers to them and take their money, and tell them what to do,' said Mrs. Brown, 'and to collect the butterflies they've done and see that they're written their names on, and then put them neatly aside for one of the Committee to judge. Do you understand, William?'

William said that he understood. They got him his little tubes of paint, pencils and paper, and he seemed very sensible about it all.

'You *do quite* understand, William, don't you?' said his mother for the hundredth time.

And William replied patiently once more that he *did quite* understand.

'And you'll be *quite* quiet?'

William promised to be *quite* quiet.

'And you'll keep Ginger and Henry and Douglas *quite* quiet?'

William promised to keep Ginger and Henry and Douglas *quite* quiet.

'I'm *sure* it will be all right,' Mrs. Brown assured the Vicar, 'he's really a very good boy, though, of course, I know that he makes mistakes sometimes.'

She was glad to feel relieved of anxiety about William's part of the entertainment, because her own part occupied all her energies. She was in charge of the teas, and, as she said pathetically to the Vicar's wife, getting cake out of people in that village was like drawing water in a sieve.

She found time, however, on the evening before the bazaar to hold a little rehearsal of the Outlaws' competition in the tent.

They stood ranged in a solemn, silent row behind the table that contained their tubes of paint, pencils and paper. Mrs. Brown entered as a competitor. They received her courteously, explained the competition to her, supervised her effort, and put her 'butterfly' away to await the judge. The whole performance was perfect, and removed the last trace of Mrs. Brown's anxiety. Her optimism, in fact, rose rather unduly considering that the day of the bazaar had not yet dawned.

'I *knew* they'd manage it all right,' she said to the Vicar's wife, who was counting out cakes with her, 'he's really *quite* sensible.'

The day of the bazaar turned out gloriously fine and almost as warm as midsummer. Workmen were busy all morning, putting up tents and marquees in the grounds. The Bishop was coming to the Hall for lunch, and the opening was to take place at two-thirty. The whole village was agog with excitement. And then news came round that increased the excitement to fever pitch. A Prominent Political Personage, motoring through the village had called at the Vicarage to ask if he might look through the church, as he was interested in Norman Architecture. The Vicar took him through the church, and told him about the bazaar that was taking place in the afternoon. The Prominent Political Person expressed interest. The news was carried to the Hall. The Prominent Political Personage was asked to come to lunch at the Hall, and to attend the bazaar afterwards. The news flew round the village. Lady Verity, the Bishop, the Prominent Political Person. It felt itself the hub of the universe.

William had been told to keep out of the way during the morning, and so implicitly did he obey orders that nothing was seen or heard of him till he appeared, clean and tidy, at the lunch table. His mother looked at him with approval.

'Now you'll remember to be quiet in your tent, won't you dear?' she said.

And William said, 'Yes, Mother,' so virtuously and earnestly that Mrs. Brown began to think that she must have misjudged him all his life, and that he must always have been like that.

Every one from the village and from all the villages around thronged the grounds of the Hall. A loud cheer arose as Lady Verity, with the Bishop on one side of her and the Prominent Political Personage on the other, came on to the lawn. They looked pleased with themselves and all the world, as those do look who have just lunched well.

The Bishop made a nice little speech, Lady Verity made a nice little speech, the Prominent Political Personage was invited to make a nice little speech, but smilingly declined.

The bazaar was pronounced open. Lady Verity, the Bishop and the Prominent Political Personage, with the Vicar hovering in the rear, went the round of the stalls.

The Prominent Political Personage bought several things at the Fancy Stall, and gave them back to be raffled. It was wonderful to see him bring out a five pound note, and stand waiting carelessly for the change.

And then he said that he really must be going, because he had a political meeting to address in London that evening. But the Bishop suddenly remembered something.

'Oh, by the way,' he said, 'wasn't some part of the entertainment to be organised by the children themselves?'

'Oh-er-yes,' said the Vicar without enthusiasm. 'Yes. Four boys are in charge of one of the competition tents.'

'We must visit that,' said the Bishop genially. He turned to the Prominent Political Personage. 'You must just visit that before you go.'

They began to make their way to William's tent. Mrs. Brown, seeing them and wishing to enjoy the proud sight of William telling a Bishop how to do a butterfly, left her tea tent, and followed in the rear. The select company entered the tent, then—stood petrified by horror and amazement.

William had from the first decided to have a show more worthy of the name than the 'Butterfly Competition' as expounded by his mother.

He and the other Outlaws had held long and earnest confabulations in the old barn on the subject, and had been from the beginning quite unanimous. Their reputation must not be compromised by such a show as the 'Butterfly Competition.' Ginger and William had paid a surreptitious visit to a neighbouring 'fair', to see which

THE SELECT COMPANY ENTERED THE TENT, AND STOOD PETRIFIED BY TERROR AND AMAZEMENT.

WILLIAM HAD DECIDED TO HAVE A SHOW WORTHY OF THE NAME.

shows were the most popular, and had returned in a state of high glee.

'We can manage all the best ones quite easily,' they had reported to the others.

And they had managed them.

At one end of the tent stood Ginger, completely naked except for a small pair of bathing drawers. But the entire contents of the tubes of paint had been used upon his skin, every inch of which was covered with indecipherable designs. Round his neck he wore a label, 'Tattood man.'

Next to him stood Henry, wearing several pillows and a hat and knitted suit of his mother's. The hat came right down over his eyes, and the knitted suit was stretched to its utmost limits.

He was labelled 'Fat Woman.'

Next to him stood Douglas, in an attitude of defiance, wearing the home-made boxing gloves, and with his stockings and shirt sleeves padded with handkerchiefs to represent muscles, labelled, 'Strong Man.'

Next to him stood William, balanced precariously upon a pair of stilts, swathed in a sheet, and labelled, 'Giant.'

William gazed complacently at his first visitors. This was a jolly sight better than what they'd expected to see. They jolly well wouldn't mind paying for *this*. Then he caught sight of his mother's face in the background. The petrified expressions on the faces of the others might possibly represent an extremity of delighted surprise, but there was no mistaking the horror on his mother's face. He started forward to explain to her. All he'd definitely promised was to be quiet, and to keep the others quiet, and he was doing that, wasn't he? And this was a jolly sight more worth paying to see than that butterfly thing, wasn't it? He started forward to explain this to her, but forgot that he was on stilts. Before he'd had time to utter a word of explanation, he overbalanced, and fell forward, clutching for support as he fell. Lady Verity and the Prominent Political Personage were in his direct line of descent. Unprepared for the sudden embrace of his outstretched arms, they lost their balance and William, the sheet, Lady Verity and the Prominent Political Personage rolled together in a glorious confusion on the floor of the tent. But a still more amazing thing happened. The white hair and moustache of the Prominent Political Personage detached itself, revealing a head and face with a likeness to the Prominent Political Personage certainly, but no more. And at the same time two miniatures—the gems of Sir George's collection—rolled out of the gentleman's overcoat.

Without waiting to claim them, he leapt to his feet,

and fled with marvellous speed and agility through the gaping crowd. There fell from him as he went several five pound notes, of the kind that he had already changed at the fancy stall.

Various details filtered through to William. The man had been identified as well known to the police. He had several times before used his likeness to the Prominent Political Personage (with the aid of wig and moustache) as a means of introduction into a country house. Scotland Yard said that he could steal a silver tea-pot under the eye of his hostess in the middle of afternoon tea without anyone's knowing that he had done it. False bank notes were merely a side line with him.

William was describing the affair to a large crowd of boys, who were hanging reverently on his words.

The affair had created a great stir among the juvenile population of the village, and William's prestige was higher than it had been for years. It was the tenth time that he had described the affair. Each time to a different audience.

His description had varied considerably each time. The first time it had been fairly accurate, the second time a little less accurate, the third time a little less accurate still. And so on. This was the tenth time.

'Well, I'll tell you jus' what happened,' said William in

his most eloquent manner. 'Well, they 'spected at Scotland Yard that this man was goin' to do this an' they din' know what to do to catch him, so they asked me an' I suggested that I'd dress up as a giant an' pretend to have a show an' then, when he came in to see it, I'd fall on him so's his wig and things would roll off an' then they'd be able to catch him. Well, they were jolly grateful to me for s'gestin' this an'—'

William had believed all his other nine versions of the affair.

But he believed this one most firmly of all.

## CHAPTER 5

# WILLIAM AND THE COW

The stable population of the village in which William lived was a small one, and every one knew every one else, but there was another population, shifting and artistic, in which William took an absorbing interest. The village and the countryside around it had the reputation of being picturesque, and so it attracted artists. These artists generally took cottages for a month or so in the summer, ignored, and were ignored by, the local population, then drifted back to town for the winter.

William usually found this shifting population more human and understanding than the ordinary all-the-year-round population. He approved of artists. Sometimes he even wondered whether to abandon one of his many future careers (such as pirate or robber chief) in favour of that of an artist. They didn't do any work. They just lounged about in the fields or woods all day in front of an easel, and their meals, which he had often shared, were unconventional picnic affairs that were much more enjoyable than the more conventional meals of his family and their friends. The only drawback to the life was that it must be dull, painting all day. William had tried painting, and, though he considered that he could paint as well as anyone, still he didn't consider that, judged as a pastime, there was much in it, and always, after experimenting with this and other careers, he returned to his original decision to be a pirate.

It was exceedingly seldom that any of the artists appeared in winter or even early spring, and so William was much surprised and interested when Honeysuckle Cottage, just outside the village, which was regularly let to artists, suddenly betrayed signs of artistic habitation in early January. There wasn't any doubt that it was artistic habitation. An easel and several canvases were being unloaded from the cab, and the lady who was supervising the unloading wore short untidy hair and no hat, and appeared almost immediately afterwards in an apple green smock, strolling about the garden, her hands in capacious pockets, whistling. William, watching her with interest through the hedge, observed that she was both young and pretty. Moreover she obviously had very good eyesight, for she suddenly spied him and called out 'Hello!'

There was no challenge or reproach in the voice. It was interested and friendly. Evidently she did not share that curious grown-up convention that you should pretend complete indifference to all your neighbours' affairs.

'Oh, do come in,' she said. 'How nice to see someone.'

William, unaccustomed to this sort of welcome from grown-ups, entered the garden slowly and cautiously.

'I was just going to explore,' went on the artist, 'and it's so dull exploring by yourself. Do you know anything about this garden?'

William, of course, knew everything about that garden. He knew indeed far more than their owners about all the gardens in the village.

'Yes,' he said still rather cautiously, for William was always cautious in his adoption of new friends.

'Well, *do* come in and help me. Is there anything interesting in it?'

William entered and, still warily at first, introduced her to her garden. His caution soon vanished. She was, as a grown-up, almost too good to be true. When she saw the open space in the middle of the little wood at the bottom of the garden, she called out, 'Oh, what a lovely place for a fire,' and when she found the little stream that ran through the end of it she said. 'Wouldn't it be fun to have races on it . . . and make a little backwater?'

The afternoon passed more quickly than William ever remembered an afternoon passing in the company of a grown-up. She said that her name was Miss Pollit, and that she'd be sketching in the field the next morning, and that he could come if he liked.

He found her already seated at her easel when he arrived. It seemed that she wanted to get the view of the copse down below the valley.

'There's a sort of purple light from the saplings that I want to get, William,' she said. 'You only get it at this time of the year.'

William received this statement with kindly indulgence. There wasn't, of course, any purple light, but he knew that all artists suffered from a defect of vision that made them see thing differently from other people.

She worked hard, and yet she could talk at the same time. She told him about things that she'd done. She'd climbed mountains in Switzerland. She'd travelled on a tramp steamer half-way round the world. She'd gone on a big game shooting expedition, and killed two lions and an elephant. William listened enthralled. When she finished he asked her breathlessly to marry him. She said that she was frightfully sorry, but she was already engaged to someone else. He made up his mind never to marry anyone, consoling himself with the reflection that, after all, a pirate was better without a wife, though he couldn't help feeling that she'd have made a splendid wife for a pirate. He went to see her every day, and the week of her visit flew by on wings. She asked him to tea on her last day.

'We'll have a fire in the wood,' she said, 'and we'll cook sausages and ham and eggs, and we'll make a lock and a backwater in the stream, and have a regatta with races on it. And I'll show you the witch doctor's bones that I got in Africa. Come in old clothes, and then we can get in as much of a mess as we want to.'

William was so much excited at this prospect that he could hardly live through the hours that intervened between the invitation and the visit.

But on the morning of the day before the visit a dreadful thing happened. Miss Pollit met him in the village and called out lightly as she passed:

'I say, I met a Mrs. Lane yesterday and she told me that her boy was a great friend of yours, so I've asked him to come too.'

Hubert Lane! Hubert Lane had been away from home for a week, but he'd come back in time to spoil what should have been the greatest day of William's life. Ever since Mrs. Lane's futile attempt to put an end to the feud between the two boys, she had, in face of all evidence to the contrary, persisted in looking upon them and referring to them as 'great friends.'

And now Hubert was coming to tea with Miss Pollit,

coming to help make a fire and cook sausages and ham and eggs, to help make a backwater and a lock in the little stream and to have races on it, and to see the witch doctor's bones that she'd brought from Africa.

The presence of Hubert, of course, would shed a blight upon every minute of it . . . It was too late to say anything. William had been struck speechless with horror, and already she was out of sight. He stood, silent and motionless, considering the situation. Impossible for her, of course, to cancel her invitation to Hubert, even if he made her understand that they were deadly foes. The only thing to do was to say nothing and go through with it, hoping for the best. Hubert might have one of his bilious attacks that day and be unable to come. Hubert had a fatal habit of over-eating, which necessitated occasional retirement from public life for a day or two. William was of an optimistic nature. There wasn't any reason why Hubert shouldn't have one of his attacks of 'gastric trouble' (as his mother called them) on the day he'd been asked to tea to Miss Pollit's. William hung about the baker's shop that morning, hoping that a particularly lurid cake that he saw upon the counter was destined for the Lanes' household. It looked the sort of cake that would incapacitate Hubert for at least three days. William, in fact, ended by fully persuading himself that Hubert would spend to-morrow in bed. He felt quite happy and secure when he rose the next day. He was sure that Hubert had eaten half the lurid cake, and was now groaning in the throes of his 'gastric trouble.'

During the morning William sauntered gaily down the road and past the Lane house. He threw a glance up at the window which he knew was Hubert's bedroom, and smiled triumphantly. But the smile was short lived, for there at the front gate stood Hubert looking revoltingly healthy, and holding a bunch of hothouse flowers tied with a ribbon.

'Look what I'm going to take to Miss Pollit, William,' he said. 'You're going' there too, aren't you?'

Hubert's small pig-like eyes gleamed with triumph. He knew that William had no hothouse flowers or indeed any flowers of any sort, and no money to buy any. Hubert always loved to go one better than anyone else. He smirked with his most nauseous friendliness as he spoke.

William walked on as if he hadn't heard him, but he walked gloomily. The whole afternoon was spoilt now. He'd been looking forward to it more than he remembered ever looking forward to anything, and now Hubert with his bunch of hothouse flowers was going to spoil every minute of it. She wouldn't like Hubert, of course, but he'd be there all the time listening, sneering, sniggering, being in fact his natural and objectionable self, storing up phrases and incidents to taunt William with from a safe distance afterwards.

William set off from home very early in the afternoon wearing his old clothes, but without the zest and eagerness that generally accompanied them. He walked indeed as slowly and dejectedly as if he had been wearing his hated Eton suit.

His dejection lasted till he reached the main street of the village, and then vanished completely at the sight of a herd of cows stampeding in all directions on meeting a charabanc. The farmer, who was in charge of them, was dancing about and waving his arms on one side of the road, and his boy doing the same on the other, while the cows scattered wildly into gardens or down side roads. Some bystanders came to the farmer's aid, and William, joining them, went in pursuit of a cow that had plunged down a narrow lane. It was, however, a more difficult task than he had foreseen. The cow ran when William ran, and walked when William walked, and William found it impossible to catch. They wandered further and further from the village. No one seemed to be following them, or to care whether William caught the cow or not. The lust of the chase, however, had entered into William's soul. He had forgotten everything but his pursuit of this elusive cow. He would catch the cow even if it took him half across England. When they had proceeded in this way for some distance, the cow seemed suddenly to tire of the game, and stood still, allowing him to come right up to it. He approached it, his heart swelling with the pride of achievement. His cow! His captured cow! He walked round it several times with a possessive swagger. He even addressed it with a mixture of propitiation and command. 'Hey, you there . . . hey, cow!' It turned its large eyes upon him. It looked as if it wanted something. Perhaps it was hungry. A heavy load of responsibility seemed to descend upon William. It was his cow. It must be fed. He gazed searchingly around him, and finally espied a haystack in a neighbouring field. He crawled through a hole in the hedge, and returned in a few minutes with an armful of hay. The cow ate it with every appearance of enjoyment. But, having eaten it, it turned its large, soulful eyes again beseechingly upon William. It must still be hungry. William set off upon another short voyage of discovery, which revealed to him a 'clamp' of turnips in a field on the other side of the road. William scrambled through the hedge and returned with an armful of turnips. His cow ate them with equal relish. William's elation knew no bounds. To have a cow of one's own, to feed it . . . He decided to be a farmer when he grew up. Then he remembered the real farmer, who was presumably awaiting his return in the village street, and, having cut a stick from the hedgerow, he gently tapped his charge with it, and turned her back again towards the village. She seemed to understand quite well what was expected of her. She ambled comfortably and slowly along the road followed by her new guardian. William marched behind her whistling, his stick over his shoulder. The cow in front of him was not one cow but thousands. He was the greatest cattle farmer in the world. All the land as far as he could see belonged to him. He was driving a huge herd of his cattle from one pasturage to another somewhere in the heart of Africa or India. The woods around were thick with Red Indians who wished to attack him and steal his cattle. They were creeping along under cover. Occasionally one or two of them would venture into the open, and then he would turn, raise his stick to his shoulder and fire, and the Red Indians would fall dead. He was the best shot in the whole world. The Red Indians had guns, too, and sometimes shot at him, but they always missed him. Thus beguiled, the road back to the village was very short. Having arrived there with his charge, he looked about him. The street was empty. No farmer, no cows, no boys, no anyone. The place wore its usual mid-afternoon 'deserted village' appearance.

William and his cow looked at each other. And suddenly William remembered his engagement. He had started off unduly early, but it was quite time now that he was on his way to Miss Pollit's. He didn't know which farm the cow belonged to, and there was no one about to ask. Well, he'd just have to leave it. Probably it would find its way home by itself. Or the farmer would come back for it. Anyway, William had done his best for it, and he couldn't be expected to do more.

Turning his back on the cow, he set off briskly towards Miss Pollit's. It wasn't till he'd gone several yards that he discovered that the cow was following him. The cow evidently considered that it belonged to him. He had fed it with hay and turnips. He had taken it into his charge. It had no intention of being left alone and ownerless in the middle of the village street. William, in order to escape the embarrassing companion, quickened his pace to a run. The cow, seeing its new friend and owner vanishing in the distance, quickened its pace to a run. William was in the terrible position of appearing to be chased by a cow. He stopped. The cow approached slowly and trustingly, obviously ready for any more contributions of hay or turnips that might be forthcoming. William considered the situation. It was, he was sure, contrary to all rules of etiquette to go out to tea accompanied by a cow. Even to Miss Pollit, who was so kind and understanding, he couldn't very well take a cow with him for tea. He tried a deep and cunning ruse. He walked for a few yards in one direction, followed by the cow, then turned swiftly and walked in the other hoping that the cow would go straight on. But the cow turned too, and continued to follow him. William sat on the bank by the roadside to consider the situation again, his head in his hands. His cow stood over him, breathing heavily down his neck. He decided finally to divest himself of all responsibility for his cow, and to go to Miss Pollit's quite independently. If the cow came too it would be its own affair. He practised the expression of detached surprise and amusement with which he should turn round at her front door as she admitted him, and say:

'I say! There's a cow just coming into your garden.'

He walked on without looking round, but he was aware from the sounds of heavy breathing and lumbering footsteps that his cow was closely following him. After turning the corner that led to Miss Pollit's cottage, he began to run in order to evade his pursuer. As he ran in at the gate, he looked back fearfully. The anxious face of his cow was just appearing round the corner. The animal broke into a trot as it saw how much the distance between them had increased. He ran up to the front door and knocked. Miss Pollit opened it.

'*Here* you are!' she said cheerfully. He entered very quickly. Just as she shut the door, he seemed to see the face of his cow appearing questingly at the front gate.

'The other boy hasn't arrived yet,' said Miss Pollit, and William's spirits sank again as he remembered Hubert.

'We won't wait for him,' went on Miss Pollit cheerfully, 'we'll go down and start the fire straight away.'

They went down to the little wood at the back of the house, and there they began to collect dry sticks for the fire.

William decided to make the most of the afternoon before Hubert came. He tried to forget everything but the glorious fact of making a fire. But he couldn't help wondering what had happened to his cow. In his search for sticks he went over to the extreme corner of the wood from which he could see the front garden, and threw a covert glance at it. Yes, his cow was there in the garden, engaged in desultorily munching the lawn and the hedge. He felt partly apprehensive, partly gratified. It was, after all, rather magnificent to go about accompanied by a cow, where other lesser mortals were accompanied by mere dogs, to have a cow waiting outside houses for one, when one went out to tea.

He came back with his little heap of gathered twigs.

Miss Pollit was bending over the fire.

'Go and see if Hubert's come, William,' she said, 'we mightn't hear the bell out here.'

William returned to the corner of the wood whence he could see the front garden. His cow had tired of the lawn, and was standing in the gateway, looking up and down the road. And just at that moment Hubert approached, walking jauntily and carrying his bouquet of hothouse flowers. He stopped, amazed to find a cow standing in the gateway, then paled and retreated hastily. It was a well known fact that Hubert was frightened of cows.

William returned to Miss Pollit.

'No, he's not come yet,' he said.

They knelt over the fire together.

'I think it's going to go now,' said Miss Pollit, 'and anyway I told his mother to tell him to come straight round to the garden, so it will be all right.'

'Yes,' said William. 'I'll get a few more sticks, shall I?'

And he returned to that fascinating corner whence he could watch the front garden. His cow had wandered from the gate now, and was standing on the lawn looking about with an expression of beneficent amusement. And once more Hubert was approaching the gate with his hothouse bouquet. He approached cautiously, his eyes fixed apprehensively upon the cow. Measuring the distance between it and the path, he was preparing fearfully to slip past on tiptoe, when the cow was suddenly moved to inspect him at closer quarters. It took a step nearer him, and with a yell he turned and fled down the road.

William returned to the fire with his armful of sticks.

'What was that noise?' said Miss Pollit.

'Oh, jus' someone on the road,' said William.

'The boy's not come yet, has he?' said Miss Pollit.

'No,' said William, 'he's not come yet.'

'The fire's going nicely now,' said Miss Pollit.

'I'll just get a few more sticks,' said William, who found the lure of that corner of the wood irresistible.

'We've got enough,' said Miss Pollit.

'Well, I'll get a few more,' said William.

'There are heaps just about here. You needn't go right over there.'

But William had already gone right over there.

'I'll help you,' said Miss Pollit, following him. Then she too looked at the front garden, and gave a little scream.

'Good heavens, there's a cow in my garden,' she said.

'So there is!' said William, as if he saw it for the first time.

'What— Oh, here's the boy,' said Miss Pollit.

For Hubert was approaching again, pale and apprehensive, holding his bouquet out as if it were a shield. The cow was eating grass at the edge of the lawn. With eyes fixed fearfully upon it, bouquet held out as if to ward it off, Hubert began to tiptoe past . . . Suddenly, just when he was opposite it, the cow looked up, mistook the bouquet for a tempting morsel, and, opening an enormous mouth, snapped it up. With a yell that could be heard from end to end of the village, Hubert fled. His yells continued, fading away into the distance as he neared his home. The cow stood munching, looking vaguely surprised, a few chrysanthemums and the white ribbon that had tied the bouquet hanging out of its mouth.

Miss Pollit was leaning against a tree, holding her sides, helpless with laughter.

'Oh, dear,' she said. 'Oh dear! Oh dear! Oh, dear! That was the funniest thing I've ever seen in my life. Was that—was that—the boy?'

'Yes,' said William, 'and he won't come back. He'll say it was a bull. He always says they're bulls.'

'He's not—*really* a friend of yours, *surely?* He didn't look—'

'No,' said William. 'He's not my friend. He's my deathly foe.'

'Oh, splendid! We won't wait for anything then now, we'll— Oh, but the cow! What shall we do about the cow?'

TO WILLIAM'S DELIGHT THE COW LOOKED UP AS HUBERT PASSED, AND MISTOOK THE BOUQUET FOR A TEMPTING MORSEL.

They had now joined the cow in the front garden, and at that moment a youth appeared at the gate with a straw in his mouth.

WITH A YELL THAT COULD BE HEARD TO THE END OF THE VILLAGE, HUBERT FLED.

He looked from them to the cow in mild reproach, and finally said:

''Ere, that's *our* cow. It's our Daisy.'

'However did it get here?' said Miss Pollit.

'Got scared in the street an' farmer sprained his ankle ketchin' 'em an' 'ad to be carried 'ome an' I took cows 'ome an' this one 'ere was missin'.'

'Well, take it,' said Miss Pollit. 'I don't want it. Do you, William?'

'No,' said William.

They watched Daisy disappear in the distance, still munching contentedly, the ribbon hanging out of her mouth. Then they turned back to the wood.

'Now,' she said, 'let's have a really jolly afternoon.'

And, his mind free of both Hubert and the cow, William had a really jolly afternoon.

## CHAPTER 6

# WILLIAM'S BIRTHDAY

It was William's birthday, but, in spite of that, his spirit was gloomy and overcast. His birthday, in fact, seemed to contribute to his gloom instead of lightening it. For one thing, he hadn't got Jumble, his beloved mongrel, and a birthday without Jumble was, in William's eyes, a hollow mockery of a birthday.

Jumble had hurt his foot in a rabbit trap, and had been treated for it at home, till William's well-meaning but mistaken ministrations had caused the vet. to advise Jumble's removal to his own establishment. William had indignantly protested.

'*Why*'s he got to go away? *Me?* I've been *curin'* him, I tell you. Well, a gipsy boy told me about that. He said, tie beech leaves round it. Well, he started chewin' off his bandage himself. I din' tell him to. Well, I wanted to try splints. I read in a book about how to put a dog's legs into splints. An' he *liked* it. He liked it better'n what he liked the bandage . . . Well, he'll prob'ly die now without me to look after him, an' it'll be your fault.'

His fury increased when his visits to the vet.'s establishment were forbidden. The vet. explained quite politely that William's presence there was having a deleterious effect upon his nerves and business.

'I din' do any harm,' said William indignantly. 'I cudn't help upsettin' that jar of goldfishes an' I din' reely start those two dogs fightin'. I bet they'd done it even if I'd not been there. An' I din' mean that white rat to get out of my pocket an' get 'em all excited. An' I din' bother him for food or anythin' when dinner-time came. I jus' ate dog biscuits an' ant eggs an' any stuff I found about.'

William's family, however, was adamant. William was not to visit the veterinary surgeon's establishment again.

'All right, he'll die,' said William with gloomy conviction, referring not to the vet., whose death would have left him unmoved, but to Jumble, 'an' it'll be all your faults, an' I hope you'll always remember that you killed my dog.'

So annoyed was he with them that, in order to punish them, he lost his voice. This, of course, alone, would have been a reward rather than a punishment, but he insisted on writing all he had to say (which was a lot) on a slate with a squeaky slate-pencil that went through everyone's head. They gave him paper and pencil, and he deliberately broke the point on the first word, and then returned to his squeaky slate-pencil to explain and apologise at agonising length. Finally, in despair, they sent over to the doctor for some medicine which proved so nauseous that William's voice returned.

This episode increased the tension between William and his family, and, when the question of his birthday celebration was broached, feeling was still high on both sides.

'I'd like a dog for my birthday present,' said William.

'You've got a dog,' said his mother.

'I shan't have when you an' that man have killed it between you,' said William. 'I've seen him stickin' his fingers down their throats fit to choke 'em, givin' 'em pills an' things. An' he puts on their bandages so tight that their calculations stop flowin' an' that's jus' the same as stranglin' 'em.'

'Nonsense, William!'

'Then why'd he stop me goin' to see 'em?' went on William dramatically. ' 'Cause he knew that I saw he was killin' 'em, chokin' 'em with givin' 'em pills an' puttin' tight bandages on 'em stoppin' their calculations flowin'. I've a good mind to go to the police. He ought to be done something to by lor.'

'You're talking a lot of nonsense, William.'

'Anyway, I want a dog for my birthday present. I'm sick

of not havin' a dog. I've not had a dog for nearly three days now. Well, even if he doesn't kill Jumble—an' he's tryin' jolly hard—an' what dog can live when he's bein' choked an' strangled all day for nearly three days—well, even if he doesn't kill him, I want another dog. I want two more dogs,' he added shamelessly, knowing that his family wouldn't give him another dog, and feeling that if he were going to have a grievance against them, he might as well have it for two dogs as one.

'Nonsense! Of course you can't have another dog.'

'I said two more dogs.'

'Well, you can't have two more dogs.'

'I'm going to give you a bottle of throat mixture for my present,' said Ethel, who had suffered more than anyone through the squeaky slate-pencil because she had been deputed to attend on him.

William glared at her.

'Yes,' he said darkly, 'you needn't think I don't know that you're trying to kill me as well as Jumble. Poisonin' *me* an' chokin' an' stranglin' *him*.'

'Would you like a party for your birthday, William?' said his mother, vaguely propitiating.

William considered this offer for a moment in silence. His mother's idea of giving a party consisted in asking back all the people who had asked him to their parties, and William knew from experience that it was impossible to move her from this attitude. He assembled in a mental review all the people who had asked him to their parties that year, and the result was a depressing one.

'I'd like a party,' he said, 'if you'll let me ask—' There followed a list of the more rowdy members of the juvenile male population of the neighbourhood. Mrs. Brown paled.

'Oh, but William,' she said, 'they're so rough, and if we give a party at all we *must* have little Susie Chambers and Clarence Medlow and all the people who've asked you—'

'Then I won't have one,' said William, 'anyone'd think it was a funeral treat you were tryin' to give me, not a birthday treat. It's not my *funeral*.'

'No, it's more likely to be ours,' said Ethel. 'I can still hear the noise of that slate-pencil.'

'I don't see how you can when it's stopped,' said William, the matter-of-fact. 'You can't hear things that aren't there to hear. At least not if you're not balmy.'

He was evidently going to elaborate this theme in relation to Ethel, but Mrs. Brown stopped him with a hasty 'That will do, William,' and William returned to a mournful contemplation of his birthday.

'You can have Ginger and Henry and Douglas to tea,'

said his mother, but it appeared that William didn't want Ginger and Henry and Douglas to tea. He explained that she always stopped them playing any interesting games when they *did* come to tea, and he'd rather go out with them and play interesting games in the fields or woods than have them to tea and get stopped every time they started an interesting game.

'Well, anyway,' he said at last, brightening, 'I needn't go to the dancing-class on my birthday afternoon.'

The dancing-class was at present the bane of William's life. He had been dismissed from one dancing-class some years ago as a hopeless subject, but Mrs. Brown, in whose breast hope sprang eternal, had lately entered him for another that was held in a girls' school in the neighbourhood. It took place on Wednesday afternoon, William's half-holiday, and it was an ever-present and burning grievance to him. He was looking forward to his birthday chiefly because he took for granted that he would be given a holiday from the dancing-class. But it turned out that there, too, Fate was against him. Of course he must go to the dancing-class, said Mrs. Brown. It was only an hour, and it was a most expensive course, and she'd promised that he shouldn't miss a single lesson, because Mrs. Beauchamp said that he was very slow and clumsy, and she really hadn't wanted to take him.

William, stung by these personal reflections, indignantly retorted that he *wasn't* slow and clumsy, and, anyway, he *liked* being slow and clumsy. And as for her not wanting to take him, he bet she was jolly glad to get him and he could dance as well as any of them if he wanted to, but he didn't believe in dancing and he never had and he never would, and so he didn't see the sense of making him go to a dancing-class, especially on his birthday. He added sarcastically that he noticed anyway that *she* (meaning Mrs. Brown) took jolly good care not to go to a dancing-class on *her* birthday.

Mrs. Brown was quietly adamant. She was paying a guinea for the course, she said, and she'd promised that he shouldn't miss any of it.

To William, wallowing with a certain gloomy relish in his ill-fortune, it seemed the worst that could possibly happen to him. But it wasn't. When he heard that Ethel's admirer, Mr. Dewar, was coming to tea on his birthday, his indignation rose to boiling point.

'But it's my birthday,' he protested. 'I don't want *him* here on my birthday.'

William had a more deeply-rooted objection to Mr. Dewar than to any of Ethel's other admirers. Mr. Dewar had an off-hand facetious manner, which William had disliked from his first meeting with him. But lately the dislike had deepened, till William's happiest dreams now took the form of shooting Mr. Dewar through the heart with his bow and arrow, or impaling him on a fence with his penknife or handing him over to the imaginary wild beasts who obeyed William's slightest behest.

For in the very early days of their acquaintance Mr. Dewar had once come upon William, dressed in his Red Indian suit, cooking an experimental mixture of treacle and lemonade in an old sardine tin over a smoking fire in the shrubbery, and since then he had never met William, without making some playful reference to the affair. 'Here comes the great chief Wild Head. Hast thou yet finished yon pale face thou wast cooking, friend?'

Or he would refer to William as 'the great chief Dark Ears,' 'the great chief Sans Soap' or 'the great chief Black Collar.' Or he would say with heavy sarcasm: 'How the flames of thy fire leapt up to the sky, great Chief! I still feel the heat of it upon my face.'

William did not consider his character of Indian Chief to be a subject for jesting, but his black looks, in Mr. Dewar's eyes, only added to the fun.

And this hated creature was coming to tea on his birthday, and would probably insinuate himself so much into Ethel's good graces that he would be coming now every day afterwards to darken William's life by his insults.

'But, William,' said his mother, 'you wouldn't have a party or anyone to tea, so you can't complain.'

'You don't want us all to go into a nunnery because it's your birthday, do you?' said Ethel.

William wasn't quite sure what a nunnery was, but it sounded vaguely like a 'monkery,' so he muttered bitterly, 'You'd suit one all right,' and went out of the room so that Ethel could not continue the conversation.

He awoke on the morning of his birthday, still in a mood of unmelting resentment. He dressed slowly and his thoughts were a sort of refrain of his grievances. A dancing-class and that man to tea on his birthday. On his *birthday*. A dancing-class and that man to tea on his *birthday*. A dancing-class and that man to *tea* on his birthday. A *dancing*-class. On his *birthday* . . .

He went downstairs morosely to receive his presents.

Ethel, of course, had not dared to give him a bottle of throat mixture. She would have liked to, because she still felt very strongly about the slate pencil, but she had learnt by experience that it was wiser not to embark upon a course of retaliation with William, because you never knew where it would lead you. So she had bought for him instead a note-book and pencil, which was as nearly an insult as she dared offer him. She assumed a very kindly expression as she presented it, and William's gloom of spirit deepened, because he had a suspicion that she meant it as an insult, and yet he wasn't sure, and it would be as galling to his pride to accept it with gratitude when she meant it as an insult, as it would be to accept it as an insult when she meant it kindly. He kept a suspicious eye upon her while he thanked her, but she showed no signs of guilt. His mother's present to him was a dozen new handkerchiefs with his initials upon each, his father's a new leather pencil-case. William thanked them with a manner of cynical aloofness of which he was rather proud.

During morning school he took a gloomy satisfaction in initiating one of his new handkerchiefs into its new life. In the course of the morning it was used to staunch the blood from William's nose after a fight in the playground, to wipe the mud from William's knees after a fall in a puddle, to mop up a pool of ink from William's desk, to swaddle the white rat that that William had brought to school with him, and as a receptable for the two pennyworth of Liquorice All Sorts that had been Ginger's present to him. At the end of the morning its eleven spotless brothers would have passed it by unrecognised.

'Now, William,' said his mother anxiously at lunch, 'you'll go to the dancing-class nicely this afternoon, won't you?'

'I'll go the way I gen'rally go to things. I've only got one way of goin' anywhere. I don't know whether it's nice or not.'

This brilliant repartee cheered him considerably, and he felt that a life in which one could display such sarcasm and wit was after all to a certain degree worth living. But still—no Jumble. A dancing-class. That man to tea. Gloom closed over him again. Mrs. Brown was still looking at him anxiously. She had an uneasy suspicion that he meant to play truant from the dancing-class.

When she saw him in his hat and coat after lunch she said again: 'William, you *are* going to the dancing-class, aren't you?'

William walked past her with a short laugh that was wild and reckless and dare-devil and bitter and sardonic. It was, in short, a very good laugh, and he was proud of it.

Then he swaggered down the drive, and very ostentatiously turned off in the opposite direction to the direction of his dancing-class. The knowledge that his mother's anxiety had deepened at the sight of this, was balm to his sore spirit. He did not really intend to play truant from the dancing-class. The consequences would be unpleasant, and life was, he considered, quite complicated enough without adding that. He walked on slowly for some time with an elaborate swagger, and then turned and retraced his steps in the direction of the dancing-class with furtive swiftness. To do so he had to pass the gate of his home, but he meant to do this in the ditch so that his mother, who might be still anxiously watching the road for the reassuring sight of his return, should be denied the satisfaction of it.

He could not resist, however, peeping cautiously out of the ditch when he reached the gate, to see if she were watching for him. There was no sign of her at door or windows, but—there was something else that made William rise to his feet, his eyes and mouth wide open with amazement. There, tied to a tree in the drive near the front door, were two young collies, little more than pups. Two dogs. He'd asked his family for two dogs and here they were. Two dogs. He could hardly believe his eyes. He stared at them, and shook himself to make sure that he was awake. They were still there. They weren't part of a dream. His heart swelled with gratitude and affection for his family. How he'd misjudged them! How terribly he'd misjudged them! Thinking they didn't care two pins about his birthday, and here they'd got him the two dogs he'd asked for as a surprise, without saying anything to him about it. Just put them there for him to find. His heart still swelling with love and gratitude, he went up the drive. As he went the church clock struck the hour. He'd only just be in time for the dancing-class now, even if he ran all the way. His mother had wanted him to be in time for the dancing-class, and the sight of the two dogs had touched his heart so deeply that he wanted to do something in return to please his mother. He'd hurry off to the dancing-class at once, and wait till he came back to thank them for the dogs. He was sure that his mother would rather he was in time for the dancing-class than that he went in now to thank her for the dogs.

He stooped down, undid the two leads from the tree, and ran off again down the drive, the two dogs leaping joyfully beside him. In the road he found the leads rather a nuisance. The two dogs ran in front of him and behind him, leapt up at him, circled round him, and finally tripped him up so that he fell sprawling full length upon the ground. When this had happened several times it occurred to him to take off their leads. They still leapt and gambolled joyfully about him as he ran, evidently recognising him as their new owner. One was slightly bigger and darker than the other, but both were very young and very lively and very lovable. Soon he grew out of breath, and began to walk. The collies began to walk, too, but had evidently preferred running. The smaller one began to direct his energies to burrowing in the ditches, and the larger one to squeeze his lithe young body through the hedge. Having squeezed it through the hedge, he found himself to his surprise in a field of sheep. He did not know that they were sheep. It was his first day in the country. He had only that morning left a London shop. But dim, wholly incomprehended, instincts began to stir in him. William, watching with mingled consternation and delight, saw him round up the sheep in the field, and begin to drive them pell-mell through the hedge into the road; then, hurrying, snapping, barking, drive them down the road towards William's house. On the way lay another field of sheep, separated by a hedge from the road. The collie plunged into this field, too, drove the occupants out into the road to join his first flock, and began to chivvy the whole jostling perturbed flock of them down the road towards William's house.

William stood and watched the proceeding. The delight it afforded him was tempered with apprehension. He had not forgotten the occasion when he had tried to train Jumble to be a sheep dog. He had learnt then that farmers objected to their sheep being rounded up and removed by strange dogs, however well it was done (and William had persisted at the time, and still persisted, that Jumble made a jolly fine sheep dog). William's mind worked quickly in a crisis. The white undulating company was already some way down the road. Impossible to bring them back. Still more impossible to separate them into their different flocks.

The collie had now made his way into a third field in search of recruits, while his main army waited for him meekly in the road. William hastily decided to dissociate himself from the proceedings entirely, to have been walking quietly to his dancing-class, and not to have noticed that one of his dogs had left him to collect sheep from all the neighbouring fields. Better to let one of his dogs go than risk losing both . . .

He hurried on to the dancing-class, occasionally turning round to throw a glance of fascinated horror at the distant sea of sheep that was still surging down the road. At their rear was William's new pet, chivvying them with gusto, his tail arched proudly like a plume.

William reluctantly turned the corner that hid the wonderful sight from him, and walked up the drive of the girls' school where the dancing-class was held. Aware of a group of little girls in dancing-frocks clustered at the downstairs window, he assumed a manly swagger, and called out curt commands to his attendant hound. ('Here, sir. To heel! Down sir!') Near the front door he tied the collie to a tree with the lead, and entered a room where a lot of little boys—most of whom William disliked intensely—

were brushing their hair and washing their hands and changing their shoes. William changed his shoes, studied his hair in the glass and decided that it really didn't need brushing, wiped his hands on his trousers to remove any removable dirt, and began to scuffle with his less sedate fellow pupils.

At last a tinkly little bell rang, and they made their way to the large room where the dancing-class was held. From an opposite door was issuing a bevy of little girls, dressed in fairy-like frills and furbelows with white socks and dancing-shoes. Followed them an attendant army of mothers and nurses, who had been divesting them of stockings or gaiters and outdoor garments. William greeted as many of these fairy-like beings as would condescend to look at him with his most hideous grimace. The one he disliked most of all (a haughty beauty with auburn curls) was given him as a partner.

'*Need* I have William?' she pleaded pitifully. 'He's so *awful*.'

'I'm not,' said William indignantly. 'I'm no more awful than her.'

'Have him for a few minutes, dear,' said Mrs. Beauchamp, who was tall and majestic and almost incredibly sinuous, 'and then I'll let you have some-one else.'

The dancing-class proceeded on its normal course. William glanced at the clock and sighed. Only five minutes gone. A whole hour of it. The longest hour of the week. And on his birthday. His *birthday*. Even the thought of his two new dogs did not quite wipe out that grievance.

'Please may I stop having William now? He's doing the steps all wrong.'

William defended himself with spirit.

'I'm doin' 'em right. It's her what's doin' 'em wrong.'

The smallest and meekest of the little girls was given to William as a partner, because it was felt that she would be too shy to protest. For some minutes she tried conscientiously to dance with William, then she said reproachfully:

'You seem to have such a lot of feet. I can't put mine down anywhere where yours aren't.'

'I've only got two,' he said distantly, 'same as other people. When I've got mine down, you should find somewhere else to put yours.'

'If I do you tread on them,' said the little girl.

'Well, you can't expect me not to have feet, can you?' said William. 'Seems to me that what you all want to dance with is someone without any feet at all. Seems to me the best way to do is for me to put mine down first,

'*NEED* I HAVE WILLIAM?' SHE PLEADED PITIFULLY.
'HE'S SO *AWFUL*.'

'I'M NOT,' SAID WILLIAM INDIGNANTLY. 'I'M NO MORE AWFUL THAN HER.'

and then you look where mine aren't and put yours there.'

They proceeded to dance on this system till Mrs. Beauchamp stopped them, and gave William another partner—a little girl with untidy hair and a roguish smile. She was a partner more to William's liking, and the dance developed into a competition as to who could tread more often on the other's feet. The little girl was unexpectedly nimble at this, and performed a sort of *pas seul* upon William's dancing slippers. He strove to evade her, but she was too quick for him. It was, of course, a pastime unworthy of a famous Indian chief, but it was better than dancing. He unbent to her.

'It's my birthday to-day and I've had two dogs give me.'

'*Oo!* Lucky!'

'An' I've got one already, so that makes three. Three dogs I've got.'

'Oo, I say! Have you got 'em here?'

'I only brought one. It's in the garden tied to a tree near the door.'

'Oo, I'm goin' to look at it when we get round to the window!'

'Yes, you have a look. It's a jolly fine dog. I'm goin' to train it to be a huntin' dog. You know, train it to fetch in the wild animals I shoot. One of the others is a performin' dog and the other's a sheep dog. They're all jolly clever. One of them's with the vet. now an' I don't know if he'll come out alive. They kill 'em as soon as look at 'em, vets. do. Chokin' 'em and stranglin' 'em. I bet what I'll do is to rescue him. Go with these other two dogs an' rescue him. I bet I can train 'em to hold the vet. down while I rescue Jumble from him. I'm not afraid of anyone and neither are my dogs.'

Mrs. Beauchamp was watching his steps with a harassed frown, and it was evident that it was only a question of seconds before she interfered.

'Not of *her* or of anyone,' said William, meaning Mrs. Beauchamp. 'Got you.'

'No, you didn't,' said the little girl, neatly withdrawing her foot from William's descending slipper and placing it firmly upon the top, 'Got *you*.'

'Well, here's the window. Have a look at my dog,' said William.

They edged to the window, and there the little girl halted, making a pretence of pulling up her socks. Then she glanced out with interest, and stood suddenly paralysed with horror, her mouth and eyes wide open. But almost immediately her vocal powers returned to her and she uttered a scream.

'*Look!*' she said. 'Oh, *look!*'

They crowded to the window—little girls, little boys, nurses and mothers.

The collie had escaped from his lead, and found his way into the little girls' dressing-room. There he had collected the stockings, gaiters and navy-blue knickers that lay about on tables and desks, and brought them all out on to the lawn, where he was happily engaged in worrying them. Remnants of stockings and gaiters lay everywhere about him. He was tossing up into the air one leg of a pair of navy-blue knickers. Around him the air was thick with wool and fluff. Bits of ravelled stockings, chewed-up gaiters, with here and there a dismembered hat, lay about on the lawn in glorious confusion. He was having the time of his life.

After a moment's frozen horror the whole dancing-class—little girls, little boys, nurses, mothers and dancing-mistress—surged out on to the lawn. The collie saw them coming and leapt up playfully, a gaiter hanging out of one corner of his mouth, and a stocking out of the other. It occurred to everyone simultaneously that the first thing to do was to catch the collie, and take the gaiter and stocking from him. They bore down upon him in a crowd. He wagged his tail in delight. All these people coming to play with him! He entered into the spirit of the game at once, and leapt off to the shrubbery, shaking his head excitedly so that the gaiter and stocking waved wildly in the air. In and out of the trees, followed by all these jolly people who were playing with him, back to the lawn, round the house, through the rose garden. A glorious game! The best fun he'd had for weeks . . .

Meanwhile William was making his way quietly homeward. They'd say it was all his fault, of course, but he'd learnt by experience that it was best to get as far as possible and as quickly as possible away from the scene of a crime. Delayed retribution never had the inspired frenzy of retribution exacted on the spot.

As he walked along the road, his brows drawn into a frown, his hands plunged into his pockets, his lips were moving as he argued with an invisible accuser.

'Well, how could I help it? Well, you gave me them, didn't you? Well, how could I know it was a dog like that? It's not done any real harm either. Jus' a few stockings an' things. Well, they can buy some more, can't they? They're cheap enough, aren't they? Grudgin' the poor dog a bit of fun! They don't mind paying as much as a pair of stockings for a bit of fun for themselves, do they? Oh no! Then why should they grudge the poor dog a bit of fun? That's all I say. An' it wasn't *my* fault, was it? I never trained him to eat stockings an' suchlike, did I? Well, I couldn't have, could I?—seein' I'd only had him a few minutes. An' what I say is—'

He turned the bend in the road that brought his own house in sight, and there he stood as if turned suddenly to stone. He'd forgotten the other dog. The front garden was a sea of sheep. They covered drive, grass and flower beds. They even stood on the steps that led to the front door. The overflow filled the road outside. Behind them was the other collie pup, his tail still waving triumphantly, running to and fro, crowding them up still more closely, pursuing truants and bringing them back to the fold. Having collected the sheep, his instinct had told him to bring them to his master. His master was, of course, the man who had brought him from the shop, not the boy who had taken him for a walk. His master was in this house. He had brought the sheep to his master . . .

His master was, in fact, with Ethel in the drawing-room. Mrs. Brown was out, and was not expected back till tea-time. Mr. Dewar considered he was getting on very well with Ethel. He had not yet told her about the two collies he had brought for her. She'd said last week that she 'adored' collies, and he'd decided to bring her a couple of them next week. He meant to introduce the subject quite carelessly when he'd reached the right stage of intimacy. He possessed the dramatic instinct and liked to produce his effects at the right moment. And so, when she told him that he seemed to understand her better than any other man she'd ever met (she said this to all her admirers in turn) he said to her quite casually:

'Oh! by the way, I forgot to mention it but I just bought a little present—or rather presents—for you this afternoon. They're in the drive.'

Ethel's face lit up with pleasure and interest.

'Oh, how perfectly sweet of you,' she said.

'Have a look at them and see if you like them,' he said.

She walked over to the window. He remained in his armchair, watching the back of her Botticelli neck, lounging at his ease—the gracious, generous, all-providing male. She looked out. Sheep—hundreds and thousands of sheep—filled the drive, the lawn, the steps, the road outside.

'Well,' said Mr. Dewar casually, 'do you like them?'

She raised a hand to her head.

'What are they for?' she said faintly.

'Pets,' said Mr. Dewar.

'*Pets?*' she screamed. 'I've nowhere to keep them. I've nothing to feed them on.'

'Oh, they only want a few dog biscuits,' said Mr. Dewar.

'*Dog* biscuits?'

Ethel stared at them wildly for another second, then collapsed on to the nearest chair in hysterics.

*

Mrs. Brown had returned home before Ethel had emerged from her hysterics. Mrs. Brown had had literally to fight her way to her front door through a tightly packed mass of sheep. If Ethel hadn't forestalled her she'd have had

'WELL,' SAID MR. DEWAR, 'LOVELY PETS, AREN'T THEY?'

ETHEL TURNED AND FACED HIM. 'PETS!' SHE SCREAMED. 'I'VE NOWHERE TO KEEP THEM.'

hysterics herself. Mr. Dewar was wildly apologetic. He couldn't think what had happened. He couldn't think how the dogs had got loose. He couldn't think where the other dog was. He couldn't think where the sheep had come from. The other dog arrived at the same moment as a crowd of indignant farmers demanding their sheep. It still had a gaiter hanging out of one corner of its mouth and a stocking out of the other. It was curveting coquettishly. It wanted someone else to play with it. William was nowhere to be seen.

William came home about half an hour later. There were no signs of Mr. Dewar, or the dogs, or the sheep. Ethel and Mrs. Brown were in the drawing-room.

'I shall never speak to him again,' Ethel was saying. 'I don't care whether it was his fault or not. I shall always connect him with that horrible moment when I looked out and saw—it was like a nightmare—nothing but sheep as far as you can see. I've told him never to come to the house again.'

'I don't think he'd dare to when your father's seen the state the grass is in. It looks like a ploughed field. You can hardly see where the beds begin, and everything in them's broken and trodden down. I shouldn't be a bit surprised if your father didn't talk of suing him.'

'As if I'd want hundreds of *sheep* like that,' said Ethel, who was still feeling distraught, and confused what Mr. Dewar had meant to do with what he had actually done. '*Pets* indeed!'

'And Mrs. Beauchamp's just rung up about the other dog,' went on Mrs. Brown. 'It evidently followed William to the dancing-class and tore up some stockings and things there. I don't see how she can blame us for that. She was really very rude about it. I don't think I shall let William go to any more of her dancing-classes.'

William sat listening with an expressionless face, as if he didn't know what they were talking about, but his heart was singing within him. No more dancing-classes . . . that man never coming to the house any more. A glorious birthday—except for one thing, of course. But just then a housemaid came into the room.

'Please, 'm', it's the man from the vet. with Master William's dog. He says he's quite all right now.'

William leapt from the room, and he and Jumble fell upon each other ecstatically in the hall. The minute he saw Jumble, William knew that he could never have endured to have any other dog beside him.

'I'll take him for a little walk,' he said; 'I bet he wants one.'

The joy of walking along the road again with his

beloved Jumble at his heels was almost too great to be endured. He sauntered along, Jumble leaping up at him in tempestuous affection. His heart was full of creamy content.

He'd got Jumble back. That man was never coming to the house any more.

He wasn't going to any more dancing-classes.

It was the nicest birthday he'd ever had in his life.

CHAPTER 7

# THE OUTLAWS AND THE HIDDEN TREASURE

'I'm going to be a millionaire when I grow up,' announced William.

'Thought you were going to be a pirate,' said Ginger.

'Thought you were going to be a lion-tamer,' said Douglas.

'Thought you were going to be an engine-driver,' said Henry.

'I'm goin' to be all those,' said William very firmly, 'but I'm goin' to be a millionaire first.'

There was a moment's silence, then Ginger said with a certain half-reluctant interest: 'How're you goin' to get to be one?'

'I've not thought about that part yet,' said William. 'You can't think of everything all at once.'

'What're you goin' to do when you are one, anyway?' said Douglas.

'I'll d'vide it with you three to start with,' said William generously. 'We'll all be millionaires.'

The interest of the others became less impersonal.

'Well,' said Ginger thoughtfully, 'well, some people *do* get to be millionaires. There's no denyin' that. An' if some people do there's no reason why we shun't.'

The logic of this seemed unanswerable.

'What'll we do with it when we've got it?' said Douglas again.

'We'll buy a decent sort of house first,' said William, 'with no carpets or anythin' like that in, so that they can't say you've made 'em muddy with not wiping your boots, an' we can break anythin' we want to 'cause it won't matter 'cause we can pay for it. I'm goin' to break ten windows every day. I bet I'll have more fun than anyone else in the world. I'm goin' to keep a window mender in my house all the time mendin' the windows ready for me to break 'em again. An' I'm not goin' to have any flowers or paths in the garden. I'm jus' goin' to let it go wild with long grass an' trees. An' I'm goin' to buy a lot of wild animals from the Zoo to live in it—elephants an' lions an' tigers an' giraffes an' things like that. All livin' wild in the garden—but we'll tame them so's they'll be tame with us but wild with everyone else. I'm not goin' to have any flowers in the garden. I never see any sense in flowers. An' I'm goin' to have a sweet shop in the house too so's we can get sweets whenever we like. We'll all be livin' together in this house. An' I'm goin' to have a real train runnin' through it all down the passages an' through the rooms, with real coals, so's we can drive it about when it's too wet to go out to play with the wild animals. I'm goin' to have switchbacks instead of staircases an' I'm goin' to have swings on the roof an' I'm goin' to have a water-chute from the roof right down to a pond in the garden. An' I'm goin' to have one room with insects all over it—snails an' caterpillars crawlin' all over the walls, so's we can watch 'em. An' they'll look a jolly sight nicer than what wallpaper does. Seems queer to me,' he ended meditatively, 'that people have been buildin' houses all these years an' never thought of a few sens'ble things like that.'

The Outlaws were silent. In imagination they were already living in this house of William's dreams, driving the train along its corridors, shooting up and down the switchback staircase, hurtling down the water-shute, breaking the windows, playing with the wild animals . . .

'An' we're goin' to have decent food to eat *too*,' went on William with great decision, 'not the sort of stuff we have to eat now. We'll have ice-cream an' ginger beer an' cream buns for every meal. Once we're millionaires we won't have any bread an' butter or rice pudding ever again all the rest of our lives . . .'

The other Outlaws, hypnotised by this picture of bliss, drew deep breaths of delight.

It was Henry who came to earth first.

'How're we goin' to start gettin' the money?' he said.

William looked at him rather coldly. William disliked being dragged too abruptly out of his dream castles.

'I wish you wun't always be in such a hurry,' he said. 'There's no sense in startin' gettin' the money till we know what we're going' to do with it, is there? There's ever so many ways of gettin' money. A rich aunt might die and leave me millions of pounds for one thing.'

'Have you got a rich aunt?' said Henry.

'No,' admitted William irritably, 'an' I wish you wun't keep on arguin'. If you're goin' to keep on arguin' all the time we shan't get much pleasure out of the money when we get it. I can't be thinkin' of everythin', at the same time, can I? I can't be thinkin' of how to get the money the same minute I'm thinkin' what to do with it. I've only got one brain same as other people, haven't I? I've told you there's hundreds of ways of gettin' to be millionaires. There—there's—' he pondered for a moment, then said with a flash of inspiration, 'there's findin' hidden treasures. Yes.' The idea, on further consideration, seemed an attractive one. 'There's findin' hidden treasure . . . Why, when you think what a lot of pirates and smugglers there must have been, the earth must be *full* of hidden treasure if you know where to dig.'

'Well, we digged for a whole afternoon once an' didn't find any,' said Douglas.

William gave a scornful laugh.

'We din' know where to look,' he said. 'Fancy anyone startin' to dig for hidden treasure without findin' a map first. It's silly to start diggin' for hidden treasure without a map.'

'Well, how do you get a map?' said Henry.

'Oh, do shut up,' said William again, irritably. 'I can't think of *everything* at the same *minute*, can I? I keep on telling you I've only got one *brain*. Anyway, it's tea-time an' I'm goin' home to tea.'

The thought of tea took the Outlaws' minds from the prospect of their future career as millionaires. They scuffled joyfully homewards down the lane, playing the informal game they always played on those occasions—a game which had no rules, and in which the sole object was to push someone else into the ditch and avoid being pushed in yourself. William was neatly precipitated into it by a combined attack from Ginger and Douglas. He landed on his head, then sat up to remove dead leaves and grass from his mouth and eyes. Ginger and Douglas, standing on the bank, braced to resist the violent onset of an avenging William, were surprised to see him remain seated in the ditch bending over something he had taken from the hedge.

'What is it?' they said, forgetting hostilities, as they bent down to see what he was doing.

'Bird's nest,' said William shortly.

He was frowning thoughtfully as he pulled the nest gently and experimentally to pieces.

A week or so ago a supercilious and æsthetically-minded friend of Robert's, whom William cordially disliked, had been holding forth on the beauty and intricate workmanship of birds' nests.

'Which of us, for all our vaunted cleverness,' he had said, 'could make a bird's nest?'

And William, intensely irritated by his manner and phraseology, had said promptly, 'I could.'

Robert's friend had adjusted his monocle, and, smiling his most superior smile, had retorted:

'On the day when you do, my dear boy, I promise you I'll eat my hat.'

Since then William had tried frequently and without success to make a bird's nest. The mental picture of Robert's æsthetic friend's eating his hat was a very pleasant one.

But even William had to admit that it was harder than it looked. He used just the same materials as the birds used—feathers, and dry grass, and moss, and even cheated a little by using glue as well, but he couldn't make them stick together in the shape of a nest.

He was examining it closely now as he took it to pieces.

'What. I don't see,' he was saying, 'is how they make the sides turn up. Seems to me . . .'

His voice died away. From among the moss and feathers he had taken a small piece of crumpled paper. He was spreading it out and examining it. Then he raised a face alight with a sort of awful joy.

'*Crumbs*!' he breathed, 'it's a map of hidden treasure!'

They tumbled down head over heels into the ditch with him, and four bullet heads battled with each other for a clearer view . . . The piece of paper was crumpled and the marks on it half obliterated, but even so it was quite plain.

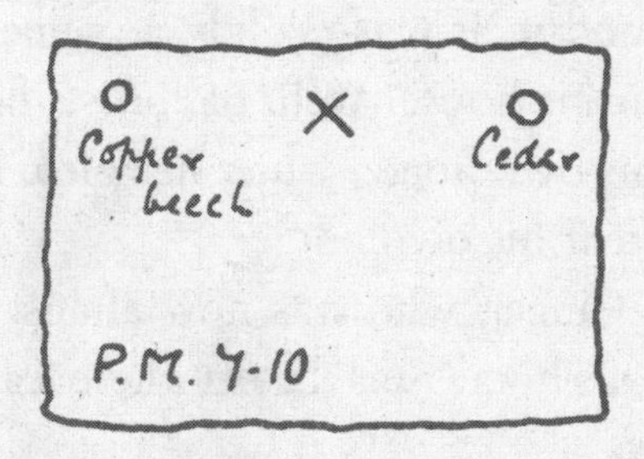


'It's the *map*,' said William, his voice still faint with excitement, 'I bet it's been in the bird's nest for hundreds an' hundreds of years. I *bet* it has. It looks old. Look at it. All yellow and old. I expect that the pirate what made it was caught by the police before he'd had time to give it to anyone, an' so he jus' threw it into the hedge when they were takin' him off to prison an' it's been here ever since . . .' He was examining it intently. 'The cross is where the treasure is, of course. They always put a cross where the treasure is.'

'But there's hundreds of copper beeches an' cedars in the world,' said Douglas. 'It would take us all our lives diggin' between every copper beech an' cedar in the world.'

'Yes,' said William eagerly, 'but he'd prob'ly made the map for his mother or wife an' they'd know which ones he meant, only of course he was caught an' took to prison before he could give it to them, an' threw it into this hedge an' a bird found it. It was prob'ly a copper beech an' a cedar jus' near his house. Well, of course, he'd be sure to bury it near his own home, wun't he? He'd *nacherally* do that, bury it near his own home.'

'Yes,' said Ginger, who was now almost as excited as William, 'an' his home *mus'* be near here 'cause of finding the paper here.'

'Yes,' shouted William, and his face shone with sudden illumination, 'there's a copper beech an' a cedar tree in Miss Peache's garden. It's the only place there's both. He must've buried it in Miss Peache's garden.'

'*Course* he must,' said Ginger, shrilly. 'An' I bet he lived at that little cottage opposite Miss Peache's. I *bet* he did. I bet he jus' slipped across at night an' buried it in Miss Peache's garden when he heard the police'd found out about him bein' a pirate, an' he'd got the map all ready to give to his mother or his wife or someone, an' they caught him before he'd had time to give it her, an' all he could do was to throw it into the hedge on the way to prison hopin' she'd find it, an' she didn't, 'cause a bird got hold of it to make its nest an''—he paused for a second to take breath and ended—'anhereitis,' all in one word.

'I say . . . I votes we sleep in tents all night in the garden with the wild animals an' have camp fires,' said Henry, his thoughts returning to their future millionaire *ménage*.

'Let's have a room full of monkeys,' said Douglas.

But William's thoughts were intent on the present.

'We've got to dig for it first,' he said slowly, 'we've got to find the 'xact spot an' dig for it. I bet it's not as easy as it looks. They never are. He must've put some catch in it, so's if anyone who wasn't his mother or wife found it they wun't be able to get hold of the treasure.'

'What does P.M. 7-10 mean?' said Ginger.

'I guess that's the catch,' said William gloomily. 'I guess that's the part that makes it hard.'

'There were witches in those days, you know,' said

Henry mysteriously, 'an' I bet they used to get witches to put spells on maps of hidden treasure. I *bet* they did. Well, if they didn't, everyone'd start diggin' an' findin' hidden treasure. I bet they paid witches to put a spell on 'em, so's only the people they meant to find 'em could find 'em. They'd give 'em sixpence for a spell for a little treasure, an' a shilling for a spell for a big one.'

The Outlaws saw no reason to disbelieve this theory. They treated the idea of fairies with incredulous scorn, but they had a wholesome respect for witches.

'Yes,' agreed William excitedly, 'I bet that was it. P.M. 7.10. That's the spell. It means ten minutes past seven in the evening . . . Well, don't you *see? That's* the spell. It means you'll only find it if you dig for it at ten past seven in the evening. *That's* it!'

'We'll do it to-night,' said Ginger hoarsely. 'We'll go there at ten past seven an' start diggin' to-night.'

William's eyes were fixed dreamily on the distance.

'Yes,' he said, 'we'll buy all the monkeys out of the Zoo an' teach 'em tricks.'

They met outside the gate of Miss Peache's house a little before ten past seven, armed with various tools. William had a garden spade, Ginger a coal shovel, Douglas a fork, and Henry the wooden spade that had been bought for his little sister at the seaside last summer. On the map the cross was placed exactly between the copper beech and the cedar, and fortunately there was a rose bed in the precise spot, which would considerably facilitate digging operations. They advanced cautiously across the lawn, and there they met their first reverse. For Miss Peache, prim and middle-aged and angular, was sitting writing at a desk at a window that overlooked the lawn. Seeing four boys trespassing in her garden, she adjusted her pince-nez and sternly motioned them away. In face of that imperious gesture they could not very well proceed with the search for hidden treasure. They returned rather disconsolately to the road.

'*Well*,' said Ginger, 'what're we goin' to do *now*?'

'We'll jus' have to wait an' try another time,' said William philosophically. 'It doesn't matter which day we do it so long as it's ten minutes past seven. We'll try to-morrow, an' if she's there to-morrow we'll try the day after, an, if she's there the day after we'll try the day after that. We'll jus' go on tryin' every day till we find a day when she's not there.'

There followed a week of daily disappointment.

Every evening at ten minutes past seven the Outlaws met outside Miss Peache's house and cautiously reconnoitred. Every day at ten minutes past seven Miss Peache was seated at her writing-table in the window, gazing abstractedly down her garden as if for inspiration.

'We can't go on for ever an' ever till she dies, goin' every night watching her looking through the window,' said Ginger eloquently. 'She might live for years and *years*. She doesn't look as if she'd ever die. Why, we may die before she does an' then what'll happen to the treasure?'

'Yes,' agreed William thoughtfully. 'We've gotter *do* somethin' now.'

'What can we do?' said Douglas dispiritedly.

'We've gotter get her away somehow. Get her away by ten minutes past seven one day, so's we can go an' find the treasure. We've gotter find out the sort of things she's int'rested in first. That's always the thing to do first—to find out what people are int'rested in.'

'How can we?' said Douglas.

'Oh, I bet we can,' said William. 'We've only got to listen to grown up people talkin'. They always talk about each other. I guess there isn't a single grown-up you couldn't find out all about by jus' listening to other grown-ups talkin'.'

'All right,' said Douglas without much hope, 'but if I know anything about grown-ups they never talk about anything you ever want to know anything about while you're there.'

But Douglas was wrong, for it was in Douglas's mother's own drawing-room that he heard Miss Peache discussed that very afternoon.

'What *does* she write?' said Douglas's mother.

'Miss Peache?' said someone. 'She writes about dreams.'

'She's *wonderful*,' said another visitor, a woman with a fringe and a very bright smile, 'simply *wonderful*. She's an *expert* on dreams. She interprets them. She knows all about what a man called Froude said about dreams.'

'I thought he was a historian.'

'Oh, no, my dear. Not a bit. He may have written histories, too, but really he's a sort of dream specialist. Tells you that they mean you had a fright as a child and that sort of thing. *Most* interesting. At present Miss Peache is making a special study of people who have *real* dreams—you know what I mean. People who dream about places and people that really exist but that they've never seen. She says that quite a lot of people do. It's wonderful to think of, isn't it? She's really marvellous, you know. She edits a magazine called "Dreams." She's a simply marvellous worker. She works every day from five to half-past seven without stopping and nothing, *nothing* is allowed to come in the way of it. She says that she sits at her desk in the window and looks at her garden for inspiration. She says that if the last trump should come between five and half-past seven it will find her there at her desk. I think it's so *wonderful*, don't you?' She turned and looked about her and ended brightly: 'And how is my dear little Douglas to-day?'

But her dear little Douglas had slipped away to impart the news to the Outlaws.

'It's *dreams* she's int'rested in,' he was saying, 'an' she's most interested of all in people that have real dreams.'

'All right,' said William in his most business-like manner, 'then we'd better start havin' real dreams.'

Miss Peache was a woman of method and habit. Every afternoon from two-thirty to three-thirty she went for her 'constitutional'. Every evening from five to seven thirty she worked in her study that overlooked the front garden. She always emerged from her gates at two-thirty to the minute, and walked through the village and up the hill, then down the hill again and through the village, reentering her gates at precisely half-past three. This afternoon she emerged from her gate as usual at two-thirty. Four boys were standing near the gate as she emerged. She could not help noticing that one of them gave a violent start of surprise on seeing her, and pointed her out to the others. Miss Peache proceeded on her way for a few yards, then looked back. The four boys were still staring after her as if transfixed with amazement. Miss Peache went a few steps farther on her way, then faltered. She was a woman of great independence and strength of mind, but those expressions of blank amazement demoralised her. Suppose she had an ink mark on her forehead, suppose her hair was coming down, suppose—she knew suddenly that she simply couldn't go on till those expressions of blank astonishment had been explained to her. She summoned an air of dignity and severity, and returned to the boys.

'What is the matter, little boys?' she said sharply, 'why are you looking at me like that? Is—is there anything *strange* about me?'

'Oh, no,' said one of them hastily. He had an earnest, freckled face, and looked transparently ingenuous. 'Oh, no. It's only that—that I *dreamed* about you last night, an' I was so surprised to see you comin' out of the gate 'cause I din' know you were a real person. I thought you were only in a dream. I'd jus' been tellin' Ginger about you in my dream, you see, an' then you came walkin' out of the gate an' I was so s'prised that I simply couldn't help looking at you like that. You see, I'd just been telling Ginger about my dream about you, and I was so surprised to find you were a real person when I thought you were only a dream that I couldn't help lookin' surprised. I'm sorry,' ended the ingenuous child smugly, 'if I was rude.'

'Not at all,' said the lady, 'not at all. This is most interesting, *most* interesting. Am I—er—exactly like the lady in your dream, my boy?'

''*Xactly*,' said her boy earnestly, 'but in my dream you hadn't got a coat on. You'd got a dress.'

'What sort of dress?' said the lady.

'A sort of—black dress with blue on it,' said the boy.

'B—but how amazing!' shrilled the lady, 'how *amazing!* I've *got* a dress like that. I was wearing it last night. How—how—how *very* amazing. *Do* tell me quickly—where was I in your dream? What was I doing? Wait a minute.'

Frenziedly the lady tore open a little handbag she carried, and took out a note-book.

'Now, my dear boy, please begin again at the very beginning.' The lady's pencil flew erratically over the paper. 'You dreamed of me—just as I am now. But in my black dress. Black with blue on it?'

'Yes,' said the boy expressionlessly, 'an' you had a long chain round your neck with a bit of glass on the end.'

'Crystal, dear, not glass,' said the lady. 'I had a crystal drop on the end of a chain. It's most amazing. Most circumstantial in every detail. Now, where was I, and what was I doing?'

'You were in a sort of room,' said William slowly; 'there was a sort of writing-table in the window and book-cases all round the room an' there was a sort of statue on one of the book-cases and there was a sort of fur rug on the floor in front of the fire and there was a sort of big blue pot umbrella-stand in a corner of the room—'

'A Nankin vase, dear,' said the lady in rather a pained voice, as she continued to scribble hard in her little note-book, 'a Nankin vase. But it's all most *amazing*. One of the most *wonderful* pieces of material that's ever come my way. Now what was I doing in your dream, my dear?'

'You were writing at the table,' said William, 'an' then someone brought you in a cup of something on a tray—'

'Coffee, my dear,' put in the lady, still writing busily, 'and what happened then?'

'You drunk it up—'

'Drank,' murmured the lady.

'And then you got up an' went to the book-shelves an' took a book out an' read it for a bit. An' then you sat down for a bit by the fire lookin' at it an' then you walked about the room again for a bit—'

'Seeking inspiration,' murmured the lady.

'YOU WERE IN A SORT OF ROOM,' SAID WILLIAM SLOWLY.

'Yes,' said William vaguely, 'seekin'—what you said. An' then you sat down and moved a vase of flowers further away from you—'

'I remember. It was unsymmetrical,' murmured the lady. 'I simply can't work where anything about me is unsymmetrical.'

'Yes,' agreed William, 'they do make an awful smell when they get like that. But they looked quite fresh to me. In the dream, I mean,' he added hastily.

'You misunderstand me, dear boy,' said the lady, 'but never mind. Continue. What did I do next?'

'You took up your pen an' put it in a sort of big silver inkpot—'

'That was presented to me, dear boy,' said the lady, still writing busily, 'by the members of a little society I was once president of. It was a little society for the interpretation of dreams. We brought our dreams to be interpreted. It was finally dissolved by ourselves because we could never agree on the interpretation of our dreams. We had, however, some very interesting and—er—animated discussions, and on the dissolution of the society the members kindly presented me with a silver inkstand. It was purchased with the money they had been collecting for the hire of a public hall for a public meeting at which we were to interpret the dreams of the public, but it was felt, perhaps rightly, that if we could not agree on the interpretation of our own dreams we should probably disagree on the interpretation of the dreams of the public. Therefore we dissolved the society. It has always been a great treasure to me. I could not work at all without it. If it were not in its place there on my writing-table I should not, I am quite sure, be able to carry on my wonderful work at all. But we are wandering from your wonderful, *wonderful* dreams, dear boy. You'd just got to where you dreamed I dipped my pen into my precious inkstand. What did I do next?'

But it was at this point that the Outlaws had left their point of vantage in the bushes near Miss Peache's window to go home to bed.

'I woke up then,' said William simply.

'Dear, dear,' said Miss Peache regretfully. 'That was a pity. Never mind. I suppose it can't be helped now . . .' She closed the little note-book, and put it back into her bag. 'Now I want you to come to me to-morrow and tell me *just* what you dream tonight. This is all most valuable material for me. *Most* valuable. It will form the basis of my next article. I think that I must forfeit my constitutional to-day to go home to write it up at once. Meet me, dear boy, at the same place and time tomorrow, and tell me exactly what you dream to-night.'

Her eyes still a-gleam with eagerness, she hurried back into the house.

*

The next day the Outlaws met Miss Peache, as arranged, just outside her house at two-thirty. It appeared that William had again dreamed about Miss Peache, but Miss Peache had this time been wearing a green velvet dress. Miss Peache's excitement at this bordered on the delirious. She *had* been wearing a green velvet dress the evening before. It was *too* wonderful. She tore out the little note-book again, quivering with eagerness, and took down verbatim William's account of his dream.

'An' then you took up the paper an' began to read it . . .'

'But I *did* do that yesterday just before I settled down to work. It's too wonderful. It really is *too* wonderful . . what did I do next, dear?'

'You took out a magazine and read that.'

'It wasn't a fiction magazine, of course, dear. It was a copy of the magazine I edit—"Dreams". I was re-reading an old article in the light of the *wonderful* experience you had described to me yesterday . . . What did I do next, dear? In your dream, of course, I mean. It tallies simply wonderfully so far with what actually happened.'

'Next,' said William, who had at the outset of the interview assumed his most bland and earnest expression and was ably maintaining it, 'next you rang the telephone.'

'And I *did*, my dear,' screamed Miss Peache. 'I

actually *did*. Oh, it's all too wonderful. *Too wonderful.* I was ringing up a dear friend of mine who is almost as deeply interested in dreams as I am to tell her about your wonderful experience, and then I—what did I do next in your dream, dear child?'

'You sat down at your table an' put your pen into your inkstand—'

'My beloved inkstand!' murmured Miss Peache fondly.

'Yes, your b'loved inkstand, then you put your hand to your head an' thought a bit—'

'I *did*,' squeaked Miss Peache, scribbling away for dear life. 'There must be some *meaning* in all this if only one could find it . . . It will probably come to us sooner or later if we just watch and wait. There's never any hurry about supernatural manifestations, you know, dear, and I always class dreams under that heading, don't you?'

William murmured quite earnestly that he did, and Miss Peache continued: 'And what did I do next, dear?'

But it had been exactly at that point that the Outlaws had realised that it was bedtime, and had crept out of the bushes whose shelter afforded them so convenient a view of Miss Peache and her room, and yet completely concealed them from her view.

'I woke up then,' said William.

'I see,' said Miss Peache. Then she said: 'Well, never

mind. It's all been most wonderful. Of course we can't *quite* see where it's leading at present, but no doubt all that will be cleared up eventually. Your dreams, dear child, have so far depicted events that have actually happened in actual surroundings. You've never dreamed of events that have not yet come to pass, but that do actually come to pass, have you, dear child?'

'N-no,' admitted William and added, 'not yet.'

'We've not got much further, have we?' said Ginger as they walked slowly homewards.

'I bet we have,' said William cryptically, 'I bet we've got a good bit further.'

But William needed all that implicit trust in Providence and in his own star that fortunately he was endowed with.

His first plan had seemed to him to be perfect, and yet it did not succeed. He retailed to Miss Peache a vivid dream in which, he said, he distinctly saw Miss Peache's study with the clock at five past seven and Miss Peache just setting off for a long walk. He added that he had a sort of *feeling* that it was a dream about the future, and that it was of an event that was going to come to pass. But Miss Peache merely smiled and said:

'Ah, no, my dear. That's quite an impossible dream. I mean, I'd never *think* of setting out for a walk during my working hours. Never *think* of it. You see, my dear, the brain gets accustomed to working at certain hours of the day, and nothing, *nothing*, should be allowed to interfere with it. I'm referring, of course, to a sensitive, highly-tuned brain such as—er—some of us are fortunate enough to possess. No, dear, I always say that two conditions are necessary for my work. I must have my beloved silver inkpot before me and I *must* have my regular hours for work. My brain is that *sensitive* order of brain that—well, that learns to work at certain hours of the day and doesn't like any alterations in those hours. You see, it lies *dormant* for the other part of the day in order to gather strength for its working hours . . . No, dear, *all* your dreams, of course, cannot be as wonderful as the ones you first told me of. This one certainly can have no meaning. Nothing *nothing* would ever induce me to set off for a walk at the hour you saw me setting off for a walk in your dream.'

William realised that he'd better go rather carefully for a bit in the matter of dreams, or Miss Peache would be losing faith in him. He decided to give dreams a rest for the time being. But still there was no doubt at all that immediate and decisive action was necessary. As Henry said, 'We can't go on like this all our *lives* with the treasure jus' near us an' not bein' able to get it. It won't be much use to us when we're ole men like we will be if we go on like this much longer.'

'Well,' said William, 'I've tried getting her out for a walk. The only other thing— *Yes!*' he exclaimed, brightening. '*That's* it. *That's* the thing to do. The thing to do is to take away her inkstand. Then she won't be able to write so p'raps she'll go out . . . Yes, *that's* the thing to try next.'

So they tried it. The abstracting of the inkpot was easier than they had imagined it would be. They merely crept through the bushes while Miss Peache was taking her afternoon's constitutional, snatched it from the table that stood at an open window, and went home with it. They concealed it at the back of a pile of firewood in a shed behind Henry's house.

But even this daring step was not immediately successful. True, Miss Peache did not write. But neither did she go out. She sat in her study ringing up the police-station every five minutes to ask if they'd had any news of her inkstand yet, and receiving messages of condolence from her friends. She spent the intervals wringing her hands, and having hysterics of a milder sort. As a spectacle the Outlaws found it highly diverting, but it did not bring them any nearer their goal of the hidden treasure. William went to Miss Peache the next morning, and described a dream in which Miss Peache busied herself continually with the telephone and wept and wrung her hands. It restored Miss Peache's faith in him completely. She explained the reason of her action.

'Now, dear boy,' she ended, 'I feel, I *really* feel, that perhaps you might *dream* where my dear inkstand is. I feel that if you fix your mind on it you *really* might. Your dreams are so wonderful, so really wonderful—all *exactly* as the things have happened evening by evening—bar that very strange one of my going out for a walk at five past seven. I haven't mentioned that one in the article I'm writing about you, dear, because it's what I can only describe as a kind of *lapse*. I'd never think of going for a walk at five past seven. But what you dreamed last night was *wonderful*—one might almost say miraculous. I expect that when you woke up you thought that it was even more impossible than the one in which I went for a walk at five past seven. It just shows, doesn't it, dear boy, that there's often some meaning in what seems to be the most *meaningless* dream. Now before you go to sleep to-night you must concentrate on finding out where my dear inkstand is. Promise me, dear boy.'

So William promised.

The Outlaws sat on the floor of the old barn and discussed the state of affairs.

Douglas was, as usual, inclined to be pessimistic.

'We shall prob'ly only get put in prison for stealin' her thing, an' they'll take the map off us while we're in prison, an' then someone else'll find the treasure an' we'll never be millionaires at all. We've took a lot of trouble an' we're not much nearer it. I feel's if I simply *couldn't* sit in that bush watchin' her again. It makes me all stiff with not bein' able to move an' earwigs an' things gettin' down my back.'

'No, we won't do that again,' said William. 'I'm gettin' a bit tired of that, too. I'm goin' to have another dream—of the future, this time—same as what she said—an' we needn't watch her for that. I'm goin' to dream of where she'll find the inkstand like what she told me to.'

'You're not goin' to dream of our shed?' said Henry anxiously.

'Oh, no, I'm not goin' to dream of that,' William reassured him. 'I'm going' to have another wrong dream, but, of course, she won't know it's wrong till she's tried. An', of course, she won't be able to blame me 'cause you can't help what you dream.'

'What's your dream goin' to be?' said Douglas, brightening.

'Well, that's what we've got to decide,' said William. 'I'm going to dream of it bein' somewhere a good long way off from her house, an' I'm goin' to dream of her findin' it at just ten minutes past seven, so's she's sure not to be in her own house at ten past seven.'

'Where are you goin' to dream she found it?' said Henry.

'Well, that's what we've got to decide,' said William. 'In a house, I should think. Then she'll be *sure* not to be able to see us in her garden. An' in a house that we know what the room's like inside, then I c'n see it in my dream.'

'An' a house of someone she knows,' said Ginger, 'then she won't mind goin' into the house to look for it.'

'I know!' said William suddenly. 'Mr Popplestone. I *know* she knows him 'cause I saw them talkin' in the road. An' his house is right at the other end of the village. An' I know what his study's like 'cause once I was in it with father.'

'Yes,' said Ginger excitedly. 'Him. Let's have him. I bet it'll be all right . . .' A far away expression came into his face. 'I say, let's have a merry-go-round in one of the rooms, the sort that makes music as it goes round.'

'You *bet* we will,' said William.

Miss Peache listened to William's dream, open-eyed and open-mouthed. At one point she threw him a suspicious glance, but the utter blankness of William's expression would have been proof against any amount of suspicious glances.

'It's—it's simply *amazing*,' gasped Miss Peache at the end, 'you say that in your dream you saw me going into Mr. Popplestone's *study?*'

'Yes,' said William, and added emphatically, 'an' it was jus' ten minutes past seven by the clock on the mantelpiece.'

'So you said before,' said Miss Peache. 'It's all so amazing. And I went to the cupboard in the wall and opened it?'

'Yes,' said William, 'you went to the cupboard in the wall and opened it—like what I said—and—'

'And found my beloved silver inkstand in it?'

'Yes,' said William, 'and found your b'loved silver inkstand in it.'

'He—he *surely* couldn't have taken it,' said Miss Peache. 'Did you—did you in your dream infer that he'd *taken* it?'

'Yes,' said William, fixing a stony stare upon his interrogator. 'That's how it seemed to me. In my dream, I mean. It seemed to me as if he'd taken it.'

'It seems so—*incredible*,' said Miss Peache faintly, 'but I've had proof, dear boy, that your dreams are not to be despised. Except on one occasion there has always been *truth* and *meaning* in your dreams. I cannot risk disobeying the clear injunction contained in the one you had last night. Er—was *he* in the room when I went to recover my inkstand? In your dream, I mean.'

William considered for a moment. He could not, of course, know whether Mr. Popplestone would be in his room when Miss Peache went to recover her inkpot, so he said very firmly:

'I don't know. I couldn't see all the room in my dream. I could only see the part of it where you found your inkpot in a cupboard in the wall. He may've been in the other part of the room or he mayn't. I cudn't see that.'

'It—it's so *extraordinary*,' said Miss Peache again. 'I'd have said that he was the last person in the world to do a thing like that. I've always considered him the soul of honour. But, of course, one knows from things one has read that some otherwise normal people are *afflicted*, as it were, in that way. Kleptomaniacs. I *hope* it's kleptomania. One knows, of course, that there *are* people living ostensibly respectable lives and in secret carrying on secret careers of crime. It would be very sad to discover that Mr. Popplestone was one of those. Very sad indeed. But still—his hobby of bird study. It may be a blind to cover his secret career. However— You said that the time by the clock was ten minutes past seven?'

'Yes,' agreed William, 'ten minutes past seven.'

'Did you—did you gather that that was important in any way. I mean did it seem what one might call vivid in any way?'

'Oh yes,' said William, with much emphasis. 'It seemed to me the most important part of the whole dream.'

'Then, of course, I must abide by it,' said Miss Peache, 'though it, as you know, is a time that as a rule I like to spend quietly in my own sanctum. I will set out this very evening at about five to seven. That will, I think, bring me there at the time you mentioned, won't it?'

'Yes,' agreed William, and nothing could have been more expressionless than the almost imbecile expressionlessness of his gaze.

Concealed in the bushes, the Outlaws watched Miss Peache, a stern avenging fury, set off from her house. Then they crept forth on to the lawn. The gardener had gone home. The maids were at the other side of the house. The coast was clear . . . Outside in the road was the wheelbarrow that they had brought to take the treasure home. They carried their spades and fork and shovel. William carried also the silver inkstand, which was to be slipped back on to Miss Peache's study table as soon as the treasure was found. They stood solemnly by the rose bed, and William took out the map, made grubbier than ever by its sojourn in his pocket.

'Here it is,' he said, 'we can't *poss'bly* be makin' any mistake. Not *poss'bly.* Here's jus' where the cross is, jus' between the copper beech an' the cedar, jus' where this rose bed is. An' we can see the church clock so the minute it gets ten past seven we'll start diggin' . . . I bet it won't take long once we start.'

Socrates Popplestone sat at his desk in his study. He had spent an enjoyable and profitable day watching a couple of whitethroats, and had sat down at his desk with the intention of writing up his notes. But he wasn't writing up his notes. He wasn't even thinking about whitethroats. He was thinking about Miss Peache. He had lately formed the habit of thinking a good deal about Miss Peache. He had admired Miss Peache from a distance for years, but he had met her on several occasions recently and found her, as it seemed, inclined to be friendly. He didn't see why—after all, she was of a very suitable age. She'd probably get over all this dream business once she was married. He'd never cared for young women. A middle-aged woman was a better companion in every way. In fact, lately, he'd begun to feel quite sentimental about Miss Peache. He'd picked up a glove that she'd left in church last Sunday, and was treasuring it as a kind of *gage d'amour.* He roused himself to begin his bird notes. He wrote the word 'Whitethroats' at the top of the page in his neat copperplate handwriting and then—a most amazing thing happened. The door opened suddenly and Miss Peache walked in. She looked quite calm and collected. She closed the door and said with dramatic quietness:

'Mr. Popplestone, you know what I've come for. I know you took it.'

A flush of guilt dyed Mr. Popplestone's cheek and brow.

His hand went to the pocket where he was carrying her glove.

'Did the verger tell you?' he asked.

He'd had a suspicion all along that the verger had seen him take it.

'No,' she said in a voice of horror, 'I'd no idea that he was a party to it. It's terrible to think of a man in a position like that—but I suppose that the position is only a cloak.' She turned to the guilty man. 'Why did you take it?' she demanded sternly.

'Because it belonged to you,' he replied.

She stared at him in amazement.

He thought that he might as well bring matters to a head.

'I've been carrying it about all day next my heart,' he went on.

'Next your h—?' she said faintly. 'Did you take the ink out of it first?'

'I never noticed any ink in it,' he said.

'You *couldn't*,' she said suddenly, 'you couldn't carry it about all day next your heart. It's too big.'

'Too big?' he said tenderly. 'If it fits your hand it can't be very big.'

'But I never put my whole hand into it . . . Oh, but why am I wasting time like this? I know where it is. A supernatural manifestation has been vouch-safed to me through a little child . . .' She walked with dramatic deliberation over to the cupboard in the wall and flung it open. In it reposed a small pile of note-books, a bottle of cough mixture, and a chest protector.

Miss Peache looked taken aback, but her moral indignation and assurance did not desert her. She pointed an accusing finger at Mr. Popplestone and said sternly: 'Where is it?'

'Here,' said the guilty man. With hanging head and cheeks suffused with a flush of shame, he brought out a crumpled white glove from his waistcoat pocket.

Miss Peache sat down suddenly on the nearest chair.

'W-w-w-what's that?' she stammered.

'Your glove,' he said simply. 'I took it on Sunday. I thought you said you'd come for it.'

'It's all so mysterious,' said Miss Peache in a faraway voice. 'I—I—I—feel rather faint, Mr. Popplestone.'

'Please call me Socrates,' said Mr. Popplestone, as he dashed wildly to the cupboard, and got out the bottle of cough mixture to restore her.

'Certainly,' murmured Miss Peache, 'and will you call me Victoria?'

Then, first making sure that they were ready to receive her, she fainted into his arms.

In the circumstances it seemed the only thing to do.

The betrothed pair entered the gate of Miss Peache's house. They had agreed to be married very quietly early the next year.

'Socrates dearest,' Miss Peache was saying anxiously, 'I *do* hope that you haven't really got a weak chest. The cough mixture and the chest protector—'

'It *is* just a little weak, Victoria,' admitted Mr. Popplestone, with a certain modest pride. 'Nothing much. Slight bronchial tendencies, that's all.'

'You want *looking* after, Socrates,' said Miss Peache fondly, 'that's what it is. Good gracious!'

She stood rooted to the spot in amazement. They had

turned the corner of the house, and there on the lawn was the astounding spectacle of four boys engaged in digging up the rose bed.

'Good gracious!' repeated Miss Peache and added faintly: 'The most extrordinary things do seem to be happening to me to-day. It's the one that has dreams too. Whatever— Boys, what are you doing?'

William had seen her, and with commendable presence of mind had thrust the silver inkstand he was carrying into the hole, covering it lightly with soil.

Then, hastily summoning his look of blank imbecility, he turned to her.

'I've just had another dream,' he said, 'I fell asleep an' I dreamed that I dug up this bed an' found your inkpot in it, so I came straight along to try.' He thrust his spade tentatively on to the ground. 'I b'lieve I've got to it at last. Yes,' he bent down and lifted it out, fixing upon Miss Peache his most earnest and candid gaze. 'Here it is.'

'How *wonderful!*' breathed Miss Peache. She turned to her fiancé. '*There.* Isn't this *proof?* You doubted the boy's veracity when I told you about him. But isn't this *proof?* And such a dear boy!'

Mr. Popplestone looked at William and saw him, not as he was, but bathed as it were in the roseate glow of the beloved's approbation. He plunged his hand into his pocket and slipped a half-crown into William's hand. It was a sort of thank-offering to Fate.

William and Ginger slipped quietly into William's mother's drawing-room, where visitors were being entertained and tea was in progress. The afternoon had been an exhausting one, and they felt too hungry to wait till their own tea time. They intended to hand round the cake-stand, and with a skill born of long practice to abstract enough cakes from it for themselves and for Douglas and Henry, who waited outside. They felt stimulated by the day's adventure. After all there was lots of time still to get the treasure. They knew where it was, anyway. They were sure they'd nearly got to it when they were disturbed. The map was still in William's pocket. They refreshed themselves with two buns from the cake-stand, and then began to listen to general conversation. Near them a woman with red hair was saying:

'Thanks so much. I simply *had* to know. She'd never forgive me if I didn't write to her this year.'

'Who?' said another woman.

'Peggy Marsden. She was so fed up with me because she said she always wrote to me for my birthday and I never wrote to her for hers. She told me to take down the date so that I shouldn't forget again, and I did, but

WILLIAM BENT DOWN AND LIFTED THE INKSTAND.
'HERE IT IS.'

I lost the bit of paper. Trixie says it's the seventh of October. I remember now. I put down P.M. 7.10 on a bit of paper to remind me. It was the bit of paper I'd begun to design Gladys's and John's new garden on. They've built a house down at Broadstairs, you know, and they were asking me to design a garden and I'd only

'HOW WONDERFUL!' BREATHED MISS PEACHE.

just begun. I'd given them a copper beech and a cedar tree and a sundial just between them, and then Peggy came in, and I made a note of her birthday on the paper and then lost it.'

William and Ginger crept brokenly out of the room. Brokenly they told the other two of the ruin of their hopes.

The four of them gazed sadly into the distance, watching their millionaire-life, described so alluringly by William, vanish into thin air.

Then William took the half-crown from his pocket, and looked at it thoughtfully.

'Well,' he said brightening a little, 'it's enough for one ice-cream an' ginger beer for us all, anyway.'

It wasn't much to salvage from the wreck of their fortunes, but it was something . . .

## CHAPTER 8

# WILLIAM THE SUPERMAN

The Outlaws, having met as usual at the corner of William's road, ambled slowly along the road to school engaged in desultory conversation.

William had propounded the question: 'What would you be if you couldn't be a yuman?' and the matter was being discussed with animation. Ginger had chosen a lion, Douglas an eagle, Henry a frog, and William a ghost, and each was heatedly defending his choice. William's choice had at first met with protest, but he had clung to it.

'*Course* a ghost's not a yuman. How could it be? Can't eat, can it? All right, nex' time I see a ghost eatin' I'll let you have it it's a yuman.'

'You've never seen a ghost at all,' objected Douglas.

'How d'you know I haven't?' said William, and added with a sound that was meant to be a sarcastic laugh, 'I've *cert'nly* never seen one eatin'.'

'Besides, it isn't eatin' that makes a yuman,' said Ginger, 'animals eat.'

'I never said it was, did I?' said William, 'all I said was you've never seen a ghost *eatin'*. Well, when you see a ghost eatin' kin'ly come'n' tell me, that's all.'

The air of triumph with which William said this made the others feel somehow that they'd got the worst of the argument.

'Anyway,' said William pursuing his advantage, 'all you'll get killed or die of starvation same as what animals do, an' I'll go on livin' for ever, jumpin' out at people an' scarin' 'em stiff. I bet I have a better time than any of you. *Lions!*' he said contemptuously to Ginger, 'they've nothin' to do all day but kill things an' eat 'em, an' I bet they have a rotten time gettin' bones an' horns' an' fur an' things in their throats. An',' his scorn deepened as he turned his gaze to Henry, '*frogs!*'

Henry felt that his choice needed defence, and began to defend it rather feebly.

'It's the splashin' I'd like,' he said, 'an' the hoppin'—great long hops.'

'Hoppin'!' said Douglas scornfully. 'What's hoppin' to shootin' through the air like what I'm goin' to do when I'm an eagle an' swooshin' down on things? Yes, an' I bet there won't be much left of *you* when you've been swooshed down on by me an' et in one mouthful.'

'Yes an' I bet you'd be jolly soon as dead as me if you

tried eatin' *me*. They don't eat frogs an' I bet it'd kill you.'

'I bet they do.'

'They don't.'

'They do.'

'They don't.'

'An' you'd better look out for me when you're foolin' about catchin' frogs,' said Ginger sternly to Douglas, 'or I'll be springin' out at you an' that'll be the end of *you*.'

'Oh *will* it,' said Douglas with spirit. 'Let *me* tell *you* that I'll be up again an' swooshin' down on *you* before you know where you are an' then there won't be much left of *you*.'

William interrupted with a sinister laugh.

'Yes, an' you all wait till I get hauntin' the wood where you all are, an' there won't be much left of any of you. You'll be scared dead with me groanin' an' moanin' an' rattlin' chains an'—'

'Yes, you'll be groanin' an' moanin' all right when I—' began Ginger, then stopped.

They had reached the school door. A procession of boys wearing grey flannel suits was streaming into it, and in the procession appeared an amazing figure—dressed in a white sailor suit with long flapping trousers, and a white sailor's cap perched on a riot of golden curls. So jauntily and assuredly did it walk that the horror plainly visible on the faces around it was paralysed into silence. It passed on its way, leaving behind it a furious medley of sounds in which indignant small boys told each other all the things they were going to say to it the next time they saw it. The Outlaws forgot their imaginary rôles in the excitement.

'Who is he?'

'What's he comin' dressed up like that for?'

'Oughter be in a baby show, that's where *he* oughter be.'

'I bet they turn him out.'

But they didn't turn him out. When the Outlaws entered their form room, he was already seated at a desk, calmly examining some books and exercise books that had been given to him by the form master. Even the form master seemed slightly disconcerted by his appearance. He explained his presence shortly to the others. His father had taken a house in the neighbourhood for a few months, and the head master had given him permission to attend the school while he was there. The head master unfortunately was not present to see the result of this permission. The head master was away with a nervous breakdown, and had left in charge the sixth form master—a muscular young man with a keen eye, upon whose notice William had always modestly shrunk from obtruding himself.

The form gazed with indignation at the white-clad curly-headed newcomer, restrained only from open demonstration by the presence of Authority. The white-clad child was wholly unmoved by their glances and comments. With an expression of the utmost complacency he settled himself down to receive—and impart—knowledge. His fluency was amazing, his French accent unexceptionable, his way with sums and problems breath-taking. The masters who visited them in the course of the morning commented on his ability, comparing it favourably with the ability of his class-mates and drawing attention to his tender years (he was, as they were repeatedly informed during the morning, two years younger than any of them). Indignation against him rose higher each moment. But all attempts to express this indignation met with failure. Grimacing at him was like grimacing at a stone wall—a stone wall moreover with an impregnable conviction of its own superiority. A threat of stronger measures was met with: 'All right. You *touch* me an' my father'll go to see your father an' *then* you'll catch it.'

There was something so suggestive of anticipatory enjoyment on the part of the white-clad child, something so calm and assured as of a prophecy often fulfilled that the would-be assailant melted away. During the next lesson, however, one of them managed to flick a large-sized ink blot on to the white sailor suit from his fountain pen when going up to write something on the board for the Latin master. On returning to his seat he sat down unsuspectingly into a little pool of ink. How it had come to be on his seat was a mystery. The white-clad child was apparently deeply absorbed in writing out the Latin for 'The General, having summoned his soldiers, gave the signal for battle.' But no one cared to experiment further upon the white suit. The Outlaws watched the newcomer with feelings of puzzled dislike, which grew stronger as the morning wore on. Their desks were too far removed from his to allow of their making personal experiment upon him, but they watched the experiments of their classmates with interest.

After school they followed him from the cloakroom to the road. The dapper, swaggering little figure had a strange fascination for them. It made its way to a large motor-car that stood in the road. A uniformed chauffeur leapt down to open the door for it. The Outlaws advanced nearer. Just as the white-clad child was about to step into the car, he turned and saw the Outlaws standing round him—an interested but hostile little group. His eyes met William's in a challenging stare.

'You'd look a bit better,' said William sternly, 'with your hair cut off.'

'An' *you'd* looka bit better,' said the amazing child without a moment's hesitation, 'with your face cut off.'

Then he stepped airily into the car and drove away, leaving the Outlaws gaping after him, open-eyed and open-mouthed.

'Well,' said William shortly, 'well, somethin' wants doin' to *him*.'

It was evident that the others were entirely in agreement with this cryptic statement.

'What *he* wants,' said Ginger vehemently, 'is the *cheek* takin' out of him. An' I votes we start by cuttin' off his hair.'

'Let's kidnap him,' said William.

'In masks,' put in Ginger eagerly.

'Take him to the old barn,' said Henry.

'Cut his hair off an' dress him in proper clothes, and burn his ole white things.'

'Wearin' masks all the time.'

'Spring out at him from somewhere, an' tie him up an' carry him off to the ole barn.'

'All wearin' masks.'

The object of the kidnapping expedition was fading

into insignificance before this sinister mental picture of four masked men leaping out of ambush . . .

'Let's hold up the car an' tie up the shofer . . .' said Ginger excitedly.

But despite their impressive vision of themselves, even Ginger felt this to be going a little too far and ended rather feebly, 'I've seen it done on the pictures, anyway.'

'No,' said William firmly. 'The shofer's not done nothin' to us. It's not fair to get him into trouble. No . . . it's this boy we've gotter kidnap. We've gotter knock some of the *cheek* out of him, that's what we've gotter do. We've gotter cut his hair off an' put some decent clothes on to him 'stead of those ole white things. I know where an ole suit of mine is what's put in the box-room ready for the rummage sale, an' I'll get it an' bring it to the ole barn an' I bet we'll knock some of the *cheek* out of him. We'll have a bonfire of his hair an' his ole white suit an' I bet he'll be scared stiff of us in masks an' things an' I bet *that'll* knock the *cheek* out of him.'

Life had been rather dull lately, and the Outlaws welcomed the prospect of an adventure.

'We'll have to think it out very carefully,' said William, 'and we'll have to keep it jolly secret, too. We don't want Scotland Yard gettin' to hear of it.'

The Outlaws agreed that they didn't want Scotland

Yard getting to hear of it, and separated, having arranged to meet the next evening after school to arrange the details of the *coup*.

But before the next evening something had happened that took William's mind entirely off kidnapping. William was not on the whole susceptible. He did not easily fall a victim to feminine wiles. There had only been one serious love passage in his life, and that had been when he had lost his heart to Joan, the little girl next door, who had long since left the neighbourhood.

Though William had forgotten her, and now treated the whole race of girls with coldness and disdain, he would occasionally meet one whose likeness to Joan would stir a tender chord in his heart. And this was what happened this afternoon. She was about William's size and she had the demure, dimpled face and dark hair that always made him think of Joan. She met William in the road, looked at him with tentative friendliness, and said, 'Hello!' It was the dimples (Joan had had them like that at the corners of her lips) that made him hesitate and finally return the greeting. He returned it scowling, in a fierce and threatening tone of voice, but he returned it, and then stood glaring at her waiting for her next move. Her next move was to dimple again and say: 'What's your name?'

He scowled more fiercely than ever, muttered 'William' and swung on his heel to walk away from her. She trotted lightly at his side. 'Mine's Angela,' she said. William unbent very slightly. 'Is it?' he said.

'Yes,' said the little girl, flattered by the interest implied in the question. 'Yes, it is . . . William, do you go to school?'

'Course,' said William gruffly.

'Do you go to the school here, William?'

'Yes.'

She clasped her hands.

'Oh, William, *William*, will you do something for me?'

William looked at her. Blue eyes, fixed on him imploringly. Dimples still faintly visible.

'A'right,' he said ungraciously. 'What?'

'Look after my little brother, William. He's gone to that school too.'

'A'right,' said William. 'A'right, I'll look after him all right.' His mind passed in a mental review the members of the junior forms, whom he treated usually with hauteur and contempt. It was going to be galling to his pride to display friendliness towards one of these inferior creatures, but—the dark eyes were fixed on him, the dimples coming and going anxiously, and William was as Samson shorn of his locks.

'A'right,' he said again, 'I'll look after him for you.'

Her gratitude was touching.

'Oh, William!' she said, 'I knew you would. I *knew* you were kind,'—William hastily assumed an imbecile expression meant to imply kindness—'and I *know* he'll be all right if *you* look after him.'

William uttered a short laugh—a laugh that hinted vaguely at a vast and sinister power.

'Oh, yes, I bet anyone's all right if *I* look after him. I bet anyone's *jolly well* all right if *I* look after him.'

'You won't let anyone be unkind to him, will you, William?'

'No,' said William, repeating his short laugh. 'No. If anyone's unkind to him they'll be jolly sorry. I bet they won't do it twice. I bet, once they know *I'm* lookin' after him. I bet there's a lot of people what'll be scared of *lookin'* at him once they know *I'm* takin' care of him.'

'Oh, *William!*'

Her eyes shone with an admiration that went to William's head like wine. His swagger became outrageous. He repeated his short laugh, which had now passed the fine point of perfection and become a rather meaningless snort.

'Then you *will* look after my little brother, William?' she repeated.

William was rather annoyed to have the little brother dragged into the conversation again. He didn't take any interest in the little brother. Again he passed the members of the junior form before his mental gaze. He hoped that it wasn't the one that squinted, or the one that howled when you looked at him. And he hoped that no one would see him speaking to the kid. And, above all, he hoped that she realised what she was asking of him.

'What's his name?' he said without enthusiasm.

'Reggie.'

The name did little to inspire confidence. If it wasn't the one that squinted, it was sure to be the one that howled.

'What's he look like?' he said. 'Does he squint?'

'Oh, *no*, William. He's *sweet*. He's a *darling*. He's got lovely curls and he always wears a white sailor suit.'

The blood in William's veins turned to ice.

'What?' he said. 'W-w-what?'

'He's sweet,' repeated Reggie's sister, 'and he's *ever* so clever, and you'll know him by his white sailor suit. Didn't you hear me say it the first time?'

William swallowed.

'No,' he said faintly, 'no, I din't quite hear the first time.'

'Well, you'll be able to recognise him now, won't you?'

'Oh, yes,' said William bitterly. 'Yes, I'll be able

to recognise him now all right.'

'He goes to school in the car because his school's farther away than mine, and I'm older. You'll know him when you see him, William. He's *ever* so sweet.'

'Oh, yes,' said William again slowly, 'I'll know him when I see him all right.'

William made his way slowly and reluctantly to the meeting at the old barn.

Alas for the fickleness of man! With his faithful band of followers William had undergone innumerable adventures, risked innumerable perils, performed innumerable deeds of daring. And at a glance from a pair of dark eyes, at the flicker of a dimple in a pair of smooth cheeks, it was all to count for nothing. William was going to meet his comrades with treachery in his heart. They turned trusting eyes on him as he entered.

'Now,' said Ginger, 'now let's make up a plan. I've found out where he's livin'. The question is where's the best place to ambush him.'

William assumed his best air of mystery.

'I've gotter plan,' he said unblushingly, 'I've gotter plan what's better'n that.'

'What is it?' said Ginger.

'I've not got it quite ready yet,' said William, 'an' I'm not goin' to tell you till I've got it quite ready.'

It is eloquent of the depths to which William had sunk that he met the trusting gaze of his followers without compunction.

'When'll you have it ready?' said Ginger.

'I don't know yet,' said William, 'an' we mustn't let him get suspicious. We mus' be all right to him so's he won't get suspicious of us. My plan won't be any good at all if he gets suspicious of us.'

It was obvious that, though still trusting, his followers were disappointed.

'I don't see what was wrong with kidnappin' him in masks,' said Ginger. 'I think that was a jolly good plan.'

'Well, wait till you hear mine,' said the perfidious William.

'Well, what *is* yours?' challenged Ginger. 'You tell us what yours is an' then p'raps we'll b'lieve it's better.'

William put on his most irritatingly superior manner.

'All right,' he said, 'if you don't want my plan, you go on an' do your own. Go on an' kidnap him. I bet you'll be sorry when you find out what my plan is.'

Even William was surprised (and, if the truth must be told, rather gratified than otherwise) at his skill in double-dealing. The assurance of his manner carried the day.

'A'right,' said Ginger meekly. 'A'right. Only I don't

see why we can't know about it now. We might be doin' somethin' to help.'

'You can,' said William. 'You can do somethin' to help. You can pretend to be nice to him. We've got to lure' (he meant lull) 'his suspicions if my plan's goin' to come off all right.'

All that evening as he moved about his home—doing his homework, sliding down the balusters, inadequately washing his hands, attending the family meals—William was conversing with the little girl. He was telling her of his heroic exploits . . . of how he had wrestled with a lion and killed it with his naked hands, how he had held at bay a hundred hostile Red Indians, armed with poisoned arrows, and how he had made his way alone and unarmed through the enemies' lines, bearded the hostile commander-in-chief in his tent, and forced him at the point of the sword to hand over all his maps and plans of battle. (William was vague as to the historical background of these exploits, but he had performed the exploits so often in imagination that the exploits themselves were more vivid than many things that had actually happened to him.)

In his mental recital of them to the little girl, he uttered his short scornful laugh so often that his father, who wasn't in a very good temper, said, 'What on earth's the matter with you? If you want to clear your throat, clear it. Don't go choking about the place like that.'

William gave him what he fondly imagined to be a crushing glance, and went out into the garden, where he told the little girl in imagination of how he had unmasked and handcuffed an international crook, whose appearance, as described by William, bore a striking resemblance to that of his father.

The next morning passed uneventfully. The white-clad child arrived in his limousine, superior and immaculate as ever. Despite the curls and white sailor suit, there was something about him that made his class-mates give him a wide berth. They hadn't forgotten the little incident of the ink pool. All except the Outlaws. The Outlaws didn't give him a wide berth. They fussed about him in revolting friendliness, occasionally getting behind him to wink at William and double up in mirth, evidently deriving intense amusement from the thought of William's secret plan in which they were assisting.

William was at the corner of the road again when the little girl returned from school, and approached her with an appearance of truculence that would have effectively concealed his feelings from any observer, but that did not seem to alarm the little girl. She greeted him eagerly.

'Oh, *William*,' she said, 'how *nice* of you.'

'I jus' happened to be here,' said William with an elaborate unconcern that defeated its own ends. 'I'd forgot that this was the time you came from school.'

'Oh, *William*, I've been *longing* to see you again. Thank you so *much*. Reggie said that all the boys were so nice to him at school, and I'm *sure* it was because of you.'

'THANK YOU SO MUCH,' SAID THE LITTLE GIRL.
'REGGIE SAID ALL THE BOYS WERE SO NICE TO HIM.'

William laughed his short, sinister laugh.

'Oh yes, it was because of me all right. I jus' told 'em they'd got to. There's not *many* people that'd dare do a thing I tell 'em not to. People that *know* me do as I tell 'em. They jolly well remember one or two things an'—' he hesitated a moment, wondering whether to introduce at this point the story of his wrestling with a lion and killing it with his naked hands, or the story of how he had held at bay a hundred hostile Red Indians, armed with poisoned arrows, or how he had made his way alone and unarmed through the enemy's lines. He'd worked them all up to such a fine pitch of perfection that he didn't want any of them to be wasted. She broke in, however, before he could introduce any of them.

'And he said that the masters were nice to him, too, but, of course, that's because he's so clever.'

Again William laughed his short sinister laugh. It was so short and so sinister now that it startled a horse looking over the fence and it fled neighing to the other side of the field.

'Oh, no,' said William. 'I bet it wasn't that. No, it wasn't *that* all right.'

His voice expressed amusement as at some dark secret.

'Oh, William, what was it then? It wasn't *you*, was it? You couldn't make the *masters* nice to him, surely?'

This seemed to amuse William intensely.

'Oh, couldn't I?' he said. 'You don't *know* the things I c'n do . . .' And he managed to get in his story of how he had made his way alone and unarmed through the enemy's lines, bearded the hostile commander-in-chief in his tent, and forced him at the point of the sword to hand over all his maps and plans of battle.

The little girl was impressed, but less impressed than by his alleged despotism over the staff of the school he attended.

'But William, the *masters*? How do you make the *masters* do what you tell them to? You can't take a sword to school.'

The mental picture thus evoked of his rising in his desk, and with drawn sword insisting on old Sparkie marking all his sums right was a pleasant one, but had to be abandoned as too difficult to substantiate.

He smiled a superior smile.

'Oh, no,' he said, 'I don't make 'em do what I want with a *sword*. Not a *sword* exactly. But I'll tell you what I did once, I was out walkin' in the jungle one day an' I suddenly heard an awful whizzin' noise, an' it was a lion leapin' down at me through the air from a tree where it'd crept to hide till I came along an' I jus' caught . . .'

But the little girl wasn't interested in the story of the

lion. She believed it implicitly, but what she was interested in—passionately, morbidly interested in—was William's terrorising of the muscular young men who formed the staff of the local Grammar School.

'But, William, the *masters!* How do you make *them* do what you want them to?'

William was rather irritated at being dragged back from the free unhampered atmosphere of the jungle to the cramped atmosphere of the school room, with young men in grey flannel suits as antagonists instead of lions.

'Oh, I jus' do,' he said vaguely, and then with a sudden inspired modesty, 'I don' talk about it. It might make other people jealous, so I don' tell people about it.'

'Oh, but, *William*. William, do tell me. William, I won't tell *anyone* how you do it. William, I *promise* you I won't. Oh, *William*, I thought I was your friend.' There was a hint of tears in her voice. William melted to it.

'I jus' *look* at 'em,' he said darkly.

'Oh, but, William, you couldn't make them do things by just *looking*.'

'Oh, cudn't I?'

William uttered his short laugh again. So short it had grown by now that the little girl threw him a glance of sympathy and said:

'Have you got hiccoughs, William? Isn't it a horrid

feeling? Hold your breath an' count twenty.'

'No,' said William coldly, 'I've not got hiccoughs, thanks.'

'Well, do tell me what you do.'

'I've told you. I *look* at 'em.'

'But, William, *looking* at them *couldn't* make them *do* things.'

'*My* lookin' at 'em does,' said William with such emphasis that he convinced both himself and the little girl.

'Oh, William, show me. Show me how you look at them.'

'I cudn't. I cudn't do it to you. It'd scare you so's you'd have nightmares every night all the rest of your life.'

'Oh, William, do *they* have nightmares every night—the masters?'

William made as if to utter his short laugh again, then thought better of it and smiled sardonically.

'I bet one or *two* of them do,' he said.

'Oh, William, do show it me. Do do it.'

He shook his head.

'No,' he said. 'I wun't do it to you. Ever. It's a norful look.'

'What sort of a look?' It was evident that the little girl took a fearful pleasure in his strange power. 'A *fierce* sort of look?'

'Yes, it's so fierce that people that've once seen it never forget it, an' what's more, they feel scared of me all the rest of their lives.'

He spoke with conviction. He was coming to believe in his Look.

'But, William, you din't ever look at the *head master* that way, did you? Not at Mr. Ferris?'

She was thrilling with delicious terror at the thought.

'He's not the real head,' said William with airy contempt.

'But did you?' she persisted.

He laughed.

'Him? I should jus' think I did. I should jus' *think* I did. He's jolly careful what he says to me now.'

'Oh, *William! Tell* me about it.'

'Oh, well. I jus' went to him . . .'

'To his house?'

'Yes, to his house. I jus' went to his house an' I walked into the room where he was sittin' . . .'

'Oh, *William!*'

'I jus' walked in the room where he was sittin' an' I stood an' looked at him.'

'With your Look?'

'Yes. With my Look. I stood an' looked at him with my Look, an' I din't say anythin' at first . . .'

William was warming to his theme. He could see the scene quite plainly.

'I jus' looked at him an' then I said: "You'd jus' better look *out* what you do to me. That's what *you'd* better do".'

'An' what did he look like?'

'Same as people do on the pictures. His mouth open an' all scrunched up.'

'Oh, I *know*. And then what happened?'

'What happened? I said: "Jus' you jolly well don't forget *that!*"'

'And what did he say?'

'Him? Huh! Nothin'. He was too scared.'

'An' after that did he leave you alone?'

'Huh! I should jolly well *think* so. He daren't speak to me or look at me now, he's so scared of me.'

'Has he never spoke to you since?'

But William was growing tired of Mr. Ferris. His Look was an idea worthy of larger scope, and already his fertile imagination was at work upon it. He was advancing stealthily upon a serried mass of Red Indians in war paint, fixing his eyes upon them with the terrible Look . . . they were dropping their poisoned arrows and turning to flee . . . He was advancing through the jungle, his head poked forward in a sinister fashion, the terrible

Look upon his face. Lions, tigers, elephants, snakes, fled in a panic-stricken stampede before him . . .

'I'll tell you somethin' I once did—' he began, but the church clock struck, and with a 'Oh, my goodness! I *shall* be late for tea,' she ran away down the road, turning at the corner to kiss her hand to him.

He stood for a moment, gazing at the spot where she had disappeared, a languishing smile on his face, but he was not allowed the enjoyment of these softer feelings for long.

Ginger, Henry and Douglas appeared at the spot where he was gazing languishingly, and his expression changed abruptly to his customary scowl.

'*Now* tell us about that plan,' they shouted as they leapt down the road to him.

The plan—he'd forgotten the plan. He gazed at them distastefully. After the little girl they looked singularly unattractive.

'What plan?' he said.

They stared at him blankly.

'*What* plan?' they repeated. 'The plan for takin' the cheek out of him an' cuttin' off his curls, of course.'

'Oh, *that*,' said William loftily. 'Well, I bet I've had other things to think of than that.'

'You've—*what?*' they said indignantly. 'But you said

you'd gotter *plan*. You told us that the beginnin' of it was to lure his suspicions, an' you'd tell us the rest when we'd done that. Well, haven't we been doin' that all mornin'? Haven't we been lurin' his suspicions, 'stead of cuttin' his hair off at once same as we wanted to, jus' 'cause of your ole plan. Well, what *is* it, that's what we want to know?'

They were staring at him mutinously. He turned on them with a ferocious grimace that was meant to represent his Look. The result was disappointing. They retorted by grimaces fiercer and more effective.

'You'd jolly well like to know what it is, wouldn't you?' he said mockingly. 'Oh, yes, I bet you'd jolly well like to know.'

'Yes, an' if you don't tell us,' said Ginger threateningly, 'we'll stop helpin' you.'

'I picked up his pencil for him to-day,' said Douglas morosely.

'An' I said good mornin' to him,' said Henry, and repeated with fierce indignation, 'Good *mornin'*. To *him*.'

'An' we're *sick* of your ole plan that never comes off,' said Ginger, 'an' if you won't tell us we'll have one on our own an' kidnap him.'

'Oh, will you!' jeered William, 'I'd jolly well like to see you.'

He felt, however, more uncomfortable than he sounded.

Though he'd never heard the phrase 'between the devil and the deep sea,' he quite appreciated its meaning.

'Yes an' we'll kidnap you, too, if you aren't careful,' said Ginger.

'Oh will you! You'll have to catch me first. Come on . . . catch me . . . Come on!'

In the exciting chase that followed all four Outlaws forgot how it had begun.

William woke up the next morning with a distinct feeling of uneasiness that was partly retrospective and partly anticipatory. Certainly the thought of the little girl and her admiration still thrilled him, but, the more he thought over what he had said to her yesterday, the more uneasy he felt. He'd definitely told her that he could assume a look that struck terror to the heart of even that redoubtable athlete Mr. Ferris. Her belief in him was touching and inspiring, but any chance might discredit his story and he could not bear the thought of losing her admiration. Moreover, there were the Outlaws clamouring for his 'plan', becoming more mutinous and turbulent every minute. How could he stop them laying violent hands upon the sacred form of Reggie, and how could he face her if they did?

Fortunately the early morning left no time to ponder on the problem, and William, flying breathlessly from his bed to breakfast and from breakfast to school—always five minutes late—was at his desk in his form room before he had time to consider the situation again.

And here the situation forced itself upon his notice in the very first period.

The mathematical master (known as Sparkie) was away with influenza, and Mr. Ferris took them for arithmetic in his place. Without exactly seeing where the danger lay, William was vaguely aware that the situation was fraught with danger. He decided that the best way of meeting it was to obliterate himself from public notice as far as possible. He applied himself earnestly to the first sum put up on the board by Mr. Ferris, which had to do with the time taken by two men to cut down eighty-eight trees at the rate of one every two hours.

'Give you an easy one to start with,' he had said with that misplaced brightness that school masters bring to bear on such subjects.

William had moved his desk slightly so that Henry's back hid him from the gaze of Authority. He sat working in an almost painful silence and immobility hardly daring to breathe lest he should bring upon himself that vague catastrophe that he felt sure the situation contained.

But he knew, of course, that Fate was not so easy to evade as that, and it was with a sinking of the heart but without surprise that he heard Mr. Ferris say:

'You, Brown, read out your answer.'

'Forty pounds, four shillings, sir,' read William in a tone of deprecating politeness.

There was a silence broken by Reggie's laugh.

It was not a laugh of honest amusement. It was a superior snigger. The acting head turned upon him.

'What's the matter with *you?*' he demanded curtly.

'Nothing sir,' said Reggie.

'What are you laughing at then?'

'That boy's answer,' said Reggie.

'All right. You can stay in an hour after school and do a few more sums as they amuse you so much.'

'I'm having a music lesson after school to-day,' objected Reggie.

'You can stay in an hour and a half to-morrow then instead.'

This sentence was greeted with subdued triumph by the form. William's delight alone was tempered by apprehension. He was very thoughtful for the rest of the day, and set off homewards promptly after afternoon school in order to avoid the meeting with the little girl. The little girl, however, was there at the corner waiting for him. He saw at once that she was distressed. She greeted him without the dimples.

'Oh, William! He says he's got to stay in to-morrow. William, he's *never* been kept in before all his life. Oh, William, *do* make him say he needn't.'

'Me?' said William faintly.

'Yes . . . Oh, William, he didn't do *anything*. They had a sum about how many days it would take some woodcutters to cut down some trees, and some *stupid* boy said pounds instead of days and Reggie laughed. Well, William, wouldn't *you* have laughed if some stupid boy had said pounds instead of days?'

'Me?' said William again feebly.

'Yes. Oh, William, I can't bear him to be kept in. He's never been kept in before. William, do make him let him off.'

'Me?' said William yet again.

'Yes . . . you know . . . You can. You *know* you can go to him an' look at him with your Look an' tell him to an' he'll have to. You *know* you can, William.'

'Yes,' said William desperately, 'I know I can, an' I wish I'd got time to but I simply haven't got time to. I'm late for tea now an' then I've got my homework an' that'll take me till bedtime so that I simply haven't got time to. An' I'm busy every *minute* to-morrow. I'm sorry an' I would if I'd got time to, but I simply haven't.'

They had been walking slowly down the road, and had

now reached the small Georgian house where Mr. Ferris lived. William observed this with secret horror, and tried to hasten past it, but the little girl had halted at the gate.

'Oh, William, it won't take you a minute. This is his house an' you can go in *now* an' ask him. William, do. William, *please* do. William, I thought you *liked* me.'

'I do,' said the goaded William. 'I tell you I *do* like you. I-I-I-don't want to go scarin' him now he's got ole Markie's work to do's well as his own. If I went scarin' him mos' prob'ly he'd have to go away for a rest cure same as old Markie, an' then there'd be no one to look after the school an' *I'd* get into trouble. Well, they might put me in prison for it an—an',' he decided that the colours might as well be laid on thick, 'an' I might die of hunger and rats crawling over me same as people in pictures.'

But this harrowing description left her unmoved.

'Oh, you couldn't, William, you *couldn't*. You needn't look at him *much*. Jus' enough to make him say that Reggie needn't stay in. You needn't frighten him dreadfully. Just do your Look. You know William. The way you do. Oh, William, do *do*, DO! William, if you don't it means that you don't love me a bit! Oh, *William!*'

William gazed into her tear-filled eyes and was lost.

'A'right,' he muttered, 'a'right, I'll go.'

'Oh, William. I *knew* you would.'

William made great play of straightening his collar and tie and pulling up his stockings. After all every second helped. Anything might happen to relieve the situation. Mr. Ferris might fall dead suddenly of heart disease, as people did in books. There continued to be no signs in the house of this sudden calamity, however, and when his tie had been straightened so that it was impossible to straighten it any more, and his stockings pulled up till it was impossible to pull them up any more, there was nothing to do but to walk slowly and draggingly up to the front door. His heart was a leaden weight in the pit of his stomach. His one comfort was that the little girl could not hear what was said at the front door.

He raised the knocker and let it fall. A housemaid appeared at the door.

William moistened his dry lips and spoke in a hoarse voice.

''Scuse me,' he said, 'but can you please tell me if Mr. Jones lives here?'

The housemaid stared at him indignantly. She saw him pass the house every morning on his way to school, and she knew that he knew quite well that Mr. Ferris lived there.

''*Course* he don't,' she said, and added threateningly, 'and get off with you!'

William got off with him as quickly as possible, assuming, however, an arrogant swagger and stern expression as he reached the road.

'I'm sorry,' he said regretfully, 'she says he's out now an' so I'm afraid I can't do it. An' I've got to be gettin' home quick now or I'll be late for tea an'—'

'But, William, he *isn't* out. I've *seen* him through the window. She was telling a story. William, *do* go again. Go an' say that you *know* he's there. Go an' *make* him say Reggie needn't be kept in. Oh William, *please*.'

Again her eyes brimmed with beseeching tears. William turned and walked very very slowly up to the front door again. He had propped the gate open in case his retreat should be a precipitous one. He raised the knocker and dropped it. The housemaid reappeared.

''Scuse me,' said William in a lifeless tone, his eyes fixed stonily upon her waistband, ' 'scuse me but I've forgotten if you said that Mr. Jones lived here or not.'

And then, just as the housemaid was opening her mouth to reply in obvious indignation, the tall and muscular figure of Mr. Ferris appeared in the passage.

'What is it?' he said sharply. 'What do you want? Come in here.'

Nightmare horror closed upon William as he entered the acting head master's study. He swallowed hard and fixed his blank gaze upon the ceiling.

'Well,' said the acting head master again, 'what is it?'

William tried to speak but his throat was dry. Then quite suddenly inspiration and his voice came to him at the same moment.

'P—please, sir,' he said, 'I-I din't quite understand one part of the lesson you gave us this mornin'.'

The acting head master threw a sharp glance of suspicion at the boy who made this astounding statement, but, though pale, the boy looked earnest enough. It was obviously no practical joke.

'Well,' he said. 'What part was it?'

His tone was not encouraging. It was the first visit of this sort he had received and he meant it to be the last.

As William's memory of the arithmetic lesson was a complete blank, it was as well that Mr. Ferris took down the book, opened it, and handed it to him.

'It was this,' said William putting his finger down at random on the page.

'It's quite simple,' said the acting head master curtly, 'you can't have been listening.'

He gave a short sharp explanation and ended:

'That's quite clear, isn't it? Good afternoon.'

William swaggered down the path to the little girl.

'Oh, *William!*' she said clasping her hands. 'Is it all right? Has he promised?'

William uttered his short sinister laugh.

'I bet I've scared him,' he said. 'I bet he'll think twice before he keeps your brother in again.'

'But William, did he say he needn't stay in tomorrow? Did he *promise?*'

'He din't *axchully* promise,' admitted William, 'but'—he assumed his swagger again—'but I bet I *scared* him all right. Huh! I bet I *scared* him. I bet everyone'll find him a bit different after *this*.'

'Oh but, William, *do* make him promise. Oh, William, I shan't sleep a minute to-night unless he axchully promises. Oh *William!*'

And such power had the beseeching eyes that before William knew what he was doing he found himself again on Mr. Ferris' door-step raising the knocker. The housemaid, who appeared almost immediately, gazed at him open-mouthed, her indignation fading into a sort of fascinated horror at this, his third appearance.

Without taking her eyes from him, she called faintly over her shoulder.

'It's that boy again, sir.'

And from the study came an irritated 'What the dickens does he want *now*? Come in here, whats-your-name!'

William entered.

'Well, what d'you want *now?*' said Mr. Ferris sharply.

William swallowed several times, and finally said in a hoarse and indistinct voice:

'Please, sir, I thought you beckoned to me from the window.'

'You thought I b—? *Get* out and if I see any more of you—'

But William was already hastening down the garden path.

''S all right,' he said in rather a shaken voice to the little girl, 'he's *axchully* promised now.'

'Oh, *William!*' Her gratitude and relief were comforting. 'Oh, William, you *are* clever. I'm *so* grateful. I'll go'n' tell Reggie now. He's been *terribly* upset. An' I'm goin' to buy a little present for him 'cause he's been so *terribly* upset. I've got sixpence. William, do come an' help me choose something for him.'

William, shaken as he was by the ordeal through which he had just passed, nevertheless showed a touching interest in Reggie's present. For William had vivid memories of a certain cake, consisting chiefly of butter cream, obtainable at the village confectioner's, that had once incapacitated him for two days. On that occasion William had eaten twelve of them at a sitting. He had, after that occasion, so completely lost the taste for them it was difficult to realise now that they had once been nectar and ambrosia to him, but still the fact remained that they had been, and there was no reason why they shouldn't be to Reggie, nor was there any reason why they shouldn't have the same effect on him as they had had on William. It was a pleasant and consoling thought . . . Reggie undergoing the agonies that had convinced William that he was on his deathbed . . . Reggie returning to school a few days later, a pale and chastened shadow of his former self. The detention would be forgotten, of course, and William would still occupy his cherished and hard-won position of hero in the little girl's heart.

'Those are the ones,' he said persuasively to the little girl, as they stood with their faces glued to the window. 'Those there. I bet he'd sooner have some of those for a present than *anything*.'

'Oh, but *William!*' she said aghast, 'they look *awful*.'

'They're not,' he assured her. 'They're *rippin'!*'

'They don't look as if they were a bit good for you.'

'Oh, but they are,' said William unblushingly. 'They're jolly good for you. If ever I'm feelin' weak, I buy some of those an' they make me feel strong again d'rectly.'

'How many shall I get?'

'Get twelve. They're a halfpenny each. Spend all your sixpence on them.'

'Oh *William!*'

'Go on. He'll be jolly grateful, I bet. They'll cheer him up like anything. I *bet* they will.'

He drew her, half reluctant, into the shop and said firmly:

'Sixpennoth of cream blodges, please. Big 'uns.'

When, leaving the little girl at her gate, he finally departed homewards, he felt more hopeful than an hour ago he would have believed possible.

The next day he got up early, and made his way to the house where Reggie and the little girl lived. He hoped to see a doctor's car at the door, but the drive was empty. He looked up at the windows hoping to see a white-clad nurse, or at any rate some signs of desperate illness, but all he saw was Reggie, leaning out of the window, be-curled and white suited as usual and looking riotously healthy. Dismay closed over him once more.

He was turning to walk thoughtfully homeward, when he heard a shout behind him, and turned to see the little girl running after him down the road.

'Oh, *William!*' she called. 'William, I was jus' comin' to your house to *tell* you. William, we're going away. William, I *hate* leaving you, but isn't it exciting?'

'Goin' away?' said William blankly.

'Yes. My daddy's got to go to America on business, an' he's got to be there for a year an' we're all goin' with him. And he's got to go at *once* and we're all going to-morrow. And we're not going to school to-day because we're going to help pack and—oh, William, if it wasn't for leaving *you* I'd be so excited. William, *do* say you'll miss me.'

'Yes, I'll miss you,' said William.

But his dismay at her news was tempered by relief. It simplified a situation that was growing too complicated even for William. After all, better lose the little girl and keep her admiration, than keep the little girl and lose her admiration.

'Reggie's sorry to leave school,' she said, 'because he's so fond of his lessons.'

William turned from a mental picture of himself as seen by the little girl to a mental picture of Reggie and the cream blodges.

'Did—did he eat them?' he said wonderingly.

'Yes,' said the little girl. 'He ate them just before supper. He *loved* them.'

'Jus'—jus' before supper?' said William feebly. 'Did—did he eat his supper after them?'

'Oh *yes*. It was his favourite supper, you see. It was trifle with lots of cream.'

Despite his curls and white suit and unbounded cheek,

there was something about Reggie that inspired unwilling respect. Twelve cream blodges and then trifle with lots of cream. The thought brought a strange unpleasant qualm even to that hard-boiled organ, William's stomach.

'Well,' he said, 'I'd better be gettin' back home to breakfast.'

'William, will you meet me to-night after school to say good-bye *properly?*'

'A'right,' said William graciously.

Reggie's absence created a certain amount of interest, which William made the most of.

'Where is he?' he said with a sinister laugh in answer to Ginger's question. 'Yes, I bet there's a lot of people would like to know that. I bet a lot of people would like to know where he is. You said I'd not gotter plan, din't you? Well p'raps you'll think a bit different now. Huh! Yes, I bet a lot of people would like to know where he is.'

This attitude was rather effective till the form master, over-officiously as William thought, explained Reggie's disappearance. Even that, however, William carried off rather well.

'Oh yes,' he said darkly, 'his father's got to go to America. Oh yes. Oh yes, an, *why's* his father got to go to America?'

'On business,' explained Henry simply.

William laughed. 'Huh! Oh yes, that's what he *says*. That's what he *says* all right. Yes, that what he *says*. Yes, I din't let you into my plan 'cause it was a bit too dangerous. Yes, it's a bit dangerous, let me tell you, gettin' a whole family drove out of a country like this. Yes, I bet you'd be s'prised if I told you some of the adventures I've had over this, but I'd said I'd get 'em drove out of the country an' I have. It takes more'n a few spies an' villains an' such-like to scare *me*.'

But even William couldn't carry it off, and, as the morning wore on and their incredulity increased, he found it necessary to resort to physical violence on the person of anyone who mentioned his 'plan.'

He still felt light-hearted with relief at Fate's intervention, however, when he went to his farewell interview with the little girl. He was rather looking forward to that last interview with her. There were some finishing touches to be put to the portrait of him that he hoped to leave in her mind.

She was waiting for him at the spot where they generally met.

'Oh, William,' she greeted him. 'It's *dreadful* saying good-bye to you. William, I've written a note saying good-bye *properly*'—she gave him a note which he slipped complacently into his pocket—'for you to read when I've gone. Oh, William, I shall think of you every single day. I do *love* you, William.'

'It's quite all right,' said William in a tone of vague politeness.

'William, Mr. Ferris came to see us this afternoon, and I thanked him for letting Reggie off staying in, though, of course, he couldn't help doing when you told him to.'

The smile froze on William's face. 'You—you said that?' he said faintly.

'Yes,' said the little girl innocently, 'and we talked about you an' how you can make people do what you want them to do by jus' lookin' at 'em. An' I said, didn't he feel *awful* the first time you went to him—the time you scared him almost to death, you know, an' said, "You jus' better look *out* what you do to *me* an' jus' you jolly well don't forget *that*".'

A strange icy sensation was playing up and down William's spine.

'You—you said that?' he said in a whisper that was only just audible.

'Yes,' said the little girl.

'An'—an' what did he say?' whispered William.

The solid earth seemed to have been cut away from under his feet. He was suspended in mid-air.

'He said, yes, he felt *awful*. I tried to make him 'scribe to me what you looked like, when you had your Look on, 'cause I told him you wouldn't do it to me 'cause of scarin' me, an' he said it was too *terrible* to 'scribe.'

William's eyes were protruding with horror, but with an almost superhuman effort he retained his fixed and ghastly smile.

'Yes,' he said. 'Well, I'd better be gettin' on or I'll be late for tea.'

He took his leave of her as in a dream, and walked homewards as in a nightmare. The only possible solution of the situation, he decided, was for the end of the world to come now at once, but William had learnt by experience that that event never takes place when summoned.

'No,' he said to himself bitterly. 'No, if it comes at all, it'll prob'ly come when I've jus' caught a fish an' before I've had time to show it to anyone, or when someone's jus' brought me an ice cream an' before I've had time to eat it,' and added, addressing the event with a fierce sardonic bitterness, 'yes, that's what you jus' *would* do.'

He entered the house gloomily.

His mother was in the kitchen, taking advantage of the cook's afternoon out to make a cake. He stood at the door, watching her morosely. It says much for the blackness of his spirit, that he made no attempt to secure any of the uncooked cake mixture for which he had a passion.

'Aren't you rather late home, dear?' said his mother. 'Mr. Ferris has just come to see your father. They're in the morning room.'

William thought that he had that afternoon plumbed the depth of horror, but he found that further depths remained, for, at this statement, it was as if his stomach had been suddenly wafted away from him, leaving a vacuum in its place.

'What's he come for?' he said at last, hoarsely.

'I don't know,' said Mrs. Brown. 'He just asked to speak to your father, and I took him in there. I do hope you haven't been getting into any mischief, William.'

Even in this ruin of William's fortune, his face mechanically assumed its look of outraged innocence.

'Me?' he said in the tone of offended surprise that, like his look of innocence, seemed to come of its own accord to meet a familiar need. 'No. 'Course not.'

He went draggingly out into the garden.

In the garden he remembered suddenly that Mr. Luton of Jasmine Villas had slipped on a banana skin in the village street and broken his leg. It was an idea . . . They couldn't do anything to you if you'd got a broken leg.

He crept into the dining-room, took a banana from a

dish on the sideboard, ate it, and carried the skin out to the garden. There he carefully laid it on a path, returned to the end of the path, then advanced jauntily, head in air. He walked over it ten times, without success. He couldn't even slip on the thing, much less break his leg on it. Next he climbed to the roof of the summer-house and fell from it, meaning to break his collar-bone. (They couldn't do anything to you if you'd got a broken collar-bone.) He landed unhurt on his feet. At this point he heard his mother calling from the front door.

'William, your father wants you.'

William shot into the tool shed like an arrow from a bow, and crouched behind the wheel-barrow.

'William!'

He didn't stir. There was silence except for the sound of his heart beating. It was beating so loud that he was afraid it would betray his hiding-place if his mother came out to look for him . . .

'William!'

That was his father. William recognised the tone of voice. He rose and dragged himself reluctantly into the morning room. His father stood by the fireplace, and Mr. Ferris sat in an arm-chair. There was a very peculiar expression on Mr. Ferris's face.

William fixed his eyes on the ceiling. His brow was

wet with perspiration. His throat was dry. His knees were unsteady.

'William,' said his father, 'Mr. Ferris tells me that you went round to his house the other evening to ask him to explain something in the Arithmetic lesson that you hadn't quite understood. He says that he's glad to see you take such an interest in your work, and he's kindly offered to give you an hour's extra Arithmetic after school every day for the next fortnight.'

Mr. Brown's voice showed his bewilderment. It was clear that that was all Mr. Ferris had told him, and that Mr. Brown was mystified. He kept trying to imagine William going round to Mr. Ferris's house to ask him to explain something in the Arithmetic class that he hadn't understood, and he couldn't. He could swallow a lot of things but he strained at that. Still—if Mr. Ferris said that it had happened, it must have happened. Perhaps they had all misjudged poor William—even the masters who gave him such execrable reports term after term. Perhaps William really took an interest in his work after all . . .

'Well, aren't you going to say thank you?' he said sharply to his son.

'Thank you, sir,' said William to the ceiling.

He simply couldn't meet that peculiar expression in Mr. Ferris's eye.

*

In the garden he climbed on to the fence to consider the situation. An hour every day for a fortnight. The only hour that was ever left when he'd finished his homework.

WILLIAM FIXED HIS EYES ON THE CEILING. HIS THROAT WAS DRY, HIS KNEES WERE UNSTEADY.

No games with his Outlaws, except at the week-end, for a fortnight. He plunged his hands into his pocket in search of consolation, and found some string, a penknife, a piece of putty, and the little girl's note. He opened it and read:

'WILLIAM,' SAID HIS FATHER, 'MR. FERRIS TELLS ME THAT YOU WENT ROUND TO HIS HOUSE THE OTHER EVENING.'

Dere William,

I think that you are the most wunderful pursun in the wurld. I shal nevver forget you.

His frown lightened despite himself.

In the little girl's imagination at any rate that sinister omnipotent figure of William's dreams would live on . . .

'William!'

It was his mother. She carried a bowl in her hands.

'William, I thought you might like to scrape this out.'

She had left a shamelessly large portion of her mixture in it, half a cake at least.

(Mrs. Brown had been most indignant at her husband's incredulity.

'Of *course* he went to Mr. Ferris because he wanted to understand his Arithmetic. Why should Mr. Ferris say he did, if he didn't? I think it's most *unfair* to William not to believe it. I've always *thought* that William must be better at his work than they make out. I've *never* believed those awful reports he gets.')

'Here you are, dear. The spoon's in it. And, William, I'm so glad that you're beginning to take such an interest in your work. I'm very much pleased about it.'

'Uh-huh!' said William modestly. She returned indoors. He scrambled down from the fence, and went to the wheelbarrow that had been left under the tree at the end of the lawn. Lying in it full length, he began slowly and with lingering relish to eat the delicious mixture. Jumble came running across the lawn, leapt upon him and sat down firmly upon his stomach. Jumble, too, loved 'raw cake,' and William divided it with him, giving them a spoonful each in turn.

Lying there in the wheelbarrow in the perfect summer evening with Jumble sitting on his stomach and this bowl of the food of the Gods in his arms, it was difficult to feel despondent, even with the prospect of that fortnight's bondage staring him in the face. After all, a fortnight has to come to an end sometime. It can't last for ever . . .

As he scraped out the last spoonful and put it into his mouth, he thought of that peculiar expression on Mr. Ferris's face—eyes twinkling, lips compressed to keep them steady—and it suddenly occurred to him that even that fortnight might not be so bad.

## CHAPTER 9

# WILLIAM PUTS THINGS RIGHT

William wandered down the road, dragging his toes in the dust. He generally did this when alone for the simple reason that he wasn't allowed to do it when with his mother. It afforded him a certain mild satisfaction, but still—he was bored.

The holidays had arrived and all his friends were away and he'd no one to play with. Even the grown-ups were of less use than usual—though grown-ups at the best of times were of little enough use—for an imminent local bazaar seemed to fill their entire horizon.

Had his friends been at home, William, of course, would have been glad that this should be so, because the Outlaws always preferred that the grown-ups should have some engrossing interest of their own; but it is difficult to devise really engrossing interests alone, and William was bored.

He had tried all the obvious resources that afternoon. He had practised with his bow and arrows till he had smashed the scullery window, and then hastened to the other end of the village, accompanied by Jumble, to establish an alibi. There Jumble, spying Miss Milton's Persian cat sunning itself in her garden, had squeezed through the hedge and returned after a short, sharp skirmish, wearing a fringe of cat's fur round his mouth.

Miss Milton's cat could be heard in the garden calling upon Heaven to witness the outrage, and, as Miss Milton was an adept in the writing of indignant notes to parents, William, dragging Jumble by the collar, hastened from the scene to establish another alibi.

He went this time into the woods for an hour's rabbiting with Jumble. Jumble, however, wasn't in a rabbiting mood, and kept bringing sticks for William to throw. William wasn't in a stick-throwing mood, and so relations became strained.

Next, William tried to play Red Indians, but Jumble wanted to play Hide and Seek instead, and, by the time William had decided to play Hide and Seek, Jumble had begun to play Red Indians, so at last William began to amuse himself by throwing stones at a tree. But the whole of creation seemed to be leagued against him because he didn't hit it once.

Then, more bored than ever, he plodded his way homewards, thinking that even a row about Miss Milton's cat or the scullery window would be preferable to another hour of his own company.

Jumble had now begun a game of his own (which seemed to consist in scratching up moss), and pretended not to hear when William told him he was going home, though he followed him casually from moss heap to moss heap as if by accident. William and Jumble adored each other, but occasionally they got on each other's nerves.

So William strolled aimlessly along the road, dragging his toes in the dust, and Jumble ferreted about in the ditch, pretending that he was out by himself. As William walked, he gazed about him, half unconsciously looking for some adventure to suggest itself. Suddenly he stopped.

A small house stood by the roadside, and behind it lay a long, narrow strip of garden. Two large beech trees stood, one on either side of the garden, at exactly the same distance from the house. One branch of each just met the other across the garden.

At once William felt that he would know no peace till he had discovered whether or not it were not possible to climb up one, cross over by those two branches that just met, and climb down the other. It might, of course, be rather difficult, because the two branches that met didn't look very strong, but still—he must find out.

He peered cautiously over the hedge. In the middle of

the lawn was a table, laid for tea, with a chair near it, but there was no human being in sight.

William crept along the hedge till he came to the beech tree. Then he began to swing himself up. Progress was rather difficult, till he reached the branches, but then it was quite easy. He climbed up to the branch that stretched across the garden and along it. Yes, he thought, it was a bit thin, but it just held him.

Here was the other branch. He had to give a little jump to get from one to the other. He gave it. He landed quite safely on the second branch, but—yes, he had been right, it *was* too thin, he thought to himself, as he hurtled through the air on to the tea-table below.

The tea-table gave way beneath him, and he sat up on the lawn in a ruin of broken table legs and smashed crockery, wondering which part of his person to rub first, and watching an interesting display of stars that seemed to be taking place around him. When that vanished, he saw to his dismay, a thin, middle-aged, rather precise-looking lady making her way down towards him from the house. He made an effort to rise, but a couple of stars knocked him on the head, and he sat down again suddenly. He was just wondering whether he could crawl to the hedge, when he saw to his amazement that the lady's face expressed only pity and concern.

'Oh, my dear boy,' she gasped, 'are you hurt?'

'*I'm* all right,' he said. 'It's stars keep hittin' me, an' I can't hit 'em back.'

She was lifting him very tenderly on to the basket chair.

'Now,' she said, 'do you feel better?'

'Yes,' said William, looking round. 'They're all gone now.' He added bitterly: 'They would. Jus' when I'm all right again an' could get at 'em.'

'No bones broken?' she faltered.

William felt himself all over with an expression copied as faithfully as possible from his family doctor.

'No,' he said at last. 'I can't *feel* any broke. I bet anyone else'd have every one broke, but I'm a jolly good faller.'

'Now you just stay there a minute,' said the lady, 'and I'll get you something to eat.'

William stayed there. Dismayed, he glanced around him at the welter of broken china and the fragments of what had once been a tea-table. He had noticed them when he first sat up after the fall, but hoped that they would clear away with the stars.

The lady reappeared with a tray on which were lemonade, iced buns, and a plate of chocolate biscuits. William's eyes glistened and his heart was struck with compunction. He had never heard the expression 'coals of fire,'—and would have considered it a very queer one if he had—but he would have appreciated its meaning at that moment. His eyes wandered again guiltily to the chaos around him.

'I'll bring you my pocket money every Sat'day,' he offered brusquely, 'till I've paid for 'em.'

'Oh, *no*, my dear boy,' said the lady. 'It was entirely my fault. Entirely.'

'Yours?' said William, amazed.

'Yes. I saw you begin to do it, and I ought to have stopped you. But, well—you know, I've *always* wondered if one could climb up one of them and down the other, and I wanted to see if you could. I know that if I'd been your age I couldn't have resisted it.'

'You?' said William.

'Yes. I was a great tree climber. I've climbed every tree in the Hall grounds. I used to live there when I was a little girl, you know.' She looked up at the trees again. 'It's not strong enough where they join, is it?'

'No,' said William. 'And you have to give a sort of jump to get from one to the other—and that does it.'

'Yes, so I saw. I'm so sorry that you hurt yourself, but I'm glad that we know quite definitely that it can't be done. And never mind those broken things. It was quite an old table, and the china can easily be replaced. I never use good china in the garden.'

'Won't you have somethin' to eat?' said William politely, passing her the buns.

'Well, you stay here and I'll bring my tea out. Are you sure you feel all right now?'

'Yes, thanks,' said William, rather regretfully. 'I feel I'd like to have a look at those stars again now, but they always go jus' when you're feelin' well enough to enjoy 'em, don't they?'

'Yes, they do,' agreed the lady. 'I often used to fall from trees when I was a little girl.'

She disappeared into the house. William sipped his lemonade and nibbled his chocolate biscuits with luxurious enjoyment. A maid came out, cleared away the broken china and table, and brought out another table and another chair.

Then the lady appeared with a tray of tea, and sat down opposite William.

'It's really very nice to have you here to tea this afternoon, dear boy,' she said, 'because I happen to be feeling rather worried.'

'Why?' said William, as distinctly as he could through half an iced bun.

'You wouldn't understand, dear,' she said with a sigh.

'I bet I would,' said William earnestly. 'I often feel like that myself.'

'Ah, but you wouldn't understand this worry,' she sighed.

'I bet I would,' said William again.

Gratitude at the unexpected kindness of his reception was swelling in his bosom, so that he was conscious of an uncomfortable sensation of constraint quite unconnected with either his fall or the iced bun. The expression of his sympathy with the lady's worry might, he thought, ease it to a certain extent.

'I bet I'd jolly well understand it,' he went on, still more earnestly, ''cause the things I worry about seem silly to other people, so I bet I'd understand about yours.'

'What sort of things do you worry about?' said the lady.

'Oh, when windows keep gettin' in the way of my arrers an' cats go stickin' their fur in Jumble's mouth an' things like that,' he said, and added truthfully: 'I don't mean that I worry a *norful* lot about them.'

'My worry,' said the lady, pouring herself out another cup of tea, 'is to do with the bazaar.'

'Yes,' said William, absent-mindedly taking a piece of the lady's bread and butter, 'yes, I've been a bit worried about that myself. When you think,' he went on, warming to his theme, 'of all the things people might have and then they go an' have—*bazaars!*'

He brought the word out with such contempt that he swallowed a mouthful of bread and butter unmasticated, and was seized with a fit of choking.

'Of course,' said the lady vaguely, patting him on the back. 'But, you see, I've had one of the fancy stalls since I was twenty. My mother always used to have one and I the other, and this was the last year I was doing it; and I *did* so want to have a good display, and I shall have nothing. Nothing at all. Take the plate to the kitchen window, dear, and the maid will give you some more buns.'

William obeyed, and returned with a fresh supply of buns. The lady refilled his glass with lemonade. Gratitude swelled again to bursting point in his bosom.

'I bet I could give you some things for your stall,' he said. 'I've got a catapult that's only broke a bit. It shoots all right. An' I'll make a bow an 'arrer for you an'—'

'No, dear,' said the lady sadly, 'it wouldn't do for a fancy stall.'

'What d'you want for a fancy stall?' said William. 'I could bring you my Sunday stockings. They've only been washed twice an' they've got fancy tops—and I could tell mother a burglar had stole 'em.'

'No, dear, thank you so much,' said the lady again. 'It's very good of you, but it really wouldn't do. You see—it's a long story and you wouldn't understand it. She thinks that it's entirely my fault that people don't call on her.'

'Who?' demanded William, mystified.

'Mrs. Porker.'

William knew Mrs. Porker. She lived at the Hall. She was large and stout and wealthy, and, though she dropped fewer aitches than her husband, she still dropped a good many.

'I used to live at the Hall before we had to sell it,' went on the lady. 'My family has lived there for hundreds of years, and, you see, people come to see me here who won't go to see her at the Hall, and she thinks it's my fault. It isn't, of course. I try to make them call on her.

'But she's very bitter about it and she dislikes me, and she's having the other fancy stall and she's asked everyone for things, even the people who generally give to me. She told them she didn't think I was having a stall this year. I dare say she really thought so, because I've been ill, and I meant to make a lot of things myself, and, having been ill, I've not been able to. And nearly all my friends seem to be abroad, and the result is I've got practically nothing, and, of course, she'll be delighted. Not that I really mind much about that, but I *did* so want to have a nice stall, and it's the last year I'm doing it. As it is, people will simply laugh at it.'

William gazed at her with a puzzled frown, as if trying hard to see the matter from her point of view.

'Yes, I see in a way,' he said at last, 'I kind of see. It's like havin' to go to school when you've not done any homework.'

'Yes,' said the lady, 'Yes. I suppose that it's something like that.'

William considered the problem in silence for a second, then brightened. 'You could pretend to be ill an' stay in bed,' he said, and added rather bitterly: '*You* could. *You've* no one to bring in the doctor to make you go to school or drink what he calls med'cine, but what tastes to *me* like poison. I never feel s'prised,' he added with a sinister laugh, 'when I hear of folks *he's* been goin' to dyin'.'

'No,' said the lady. 'I couldn't do that. It wouldn't seem quite honest to me, somehow.'

'It always seems quite honest to me,' William assured her.

'Yes, of course,' she said. 'I'm sure it is honest to you, because—well, of course, your parents ought to know whether you're really ill or not; but with me it's different.'

This moral distinction was too subtle for William. He shook his head with a puzzled frown.

'The only difference I can see is that it's easier for you,' he said. 'Anyway, that's what I'd do. An' I'll help you if you like. I'll tell people that I saw you fall downstairs an' break your leg. An I'll say that you're not havin' any doctors, 'cause you don't like 'em or—' His face beamed with sudden inspiration. 'I say! How'd it be if I put on a false beard (Robert's got one), an' a hat an' coat of father's an' came in pretending to be a doctor?'

'Oh, no!' said the lady, laughing. 'No, it wouldn't do at all. But it's very kind of you to think of it. Very kind indeed. And now I suppose you ought to be going home.'

William rose reluctantly. He would have been quite happy to have spent the rest of the afternoon talking to the lady and eating iced buns.

'Thanks awfully,' he said as he took his departure, 'an' you leave all that fancy stall stuff to me. I bet I get you some things for it.'

The lady thanked him very politely, and he set off down the road.

In his breath was a fierce determination to stock the lady's fancy stall for her, regardless of consequences to himself. His first efforts were unsuccessful. He met a small boy returning from the Kindergarten with the result of a day's work, in the shape of a kettle-holder, in his hands.

He was a credulous child, and William soon induced him to part with the kettle-holder in exchange for an acorn, which, William affirmed, had magic properties and would protect him from the witches and wizards of which, William further assured him, the neighbouring woods were full. The child walked on happily, carrying the acorn, and William walked on happily, carrying the kettle-holder. But this peaceful picture was shattered by the advent of the child's mother, who had heard its story with indignation and immediately set off in pursuit of William.

She overtook him, retrieved the kettle-holder, announcing at the same time her intention of teaching him to interfere with their 'Erbert again. The lesson, as far as William was concerned, took the form of a sharp impact of the lady's hand upon the side of his head, which precipitated him into the ditch and caused another, but milder, display of heavenly bodies.

He climbed out of the ditch with slow dignity and fixed a stern eye upon 'Erbert, who was watching proceedings with a mixture of delight and anxiety.

'Well, don't blame me *now* if they get you,' he said ominously, and set off at full speed down the road, pursued by 'Erbert's sobs and the threats of 'Erbert's infuriated mother.

At home he found a visitor having tea with his mother. As the buns and chocolate biscuits and lemonade he had eaten were now but a memory, he washed his face and hands (without undue attention to detail), inadequately smoothed back his hair, and descended to the hall.

Then he entered the drawing-room, and, regardless of the fact that both their plates were full, began to hand the cake-stand to his mother and the visitor, with a flourish that made his mother close her eyes in silent prayer for her best cake plates. Then he sat down, and fixed his eyes meaningly on his mother, moving them occasionally to the cake-stand.

His mother looked at him helplessly.

'Your tea will be ready in the dining-room at five, dear,' she said at last, 'but you may have a piece of bread and butter now if you like.'

'Thanks,' said William apologetically. 'It does sort of seem a long time between lunch and tea.' Giving a wide interpretation to the words 'bread and butter,' he took the largest piece of cake he could see after a fairly lengthy inspection.

'Yes, dear,' said Mrs. Brown hastily to the visitor, wishing to turn her attention from the phenomenon of William engaged in eating cake.

'Oh, I was talking about Mrs. Porker,' said the visitor,

drawing her eyes with reluctance from the fascinating sight. 'Such a ridiculous woman! You remember that dreadful little dog of hers? The shape of a football and so bad-tempered that no one could go near it? It used to sit at table with her at every meal and have chicken, always freshly cooked, because it didn't like twice-cooked meat.

'Well, it died last week, and the woman's going about in deep mourning. She's having the other fancy stall at the bazaar, you know. Such hard lines on Miss Rossiter. She's got simply nothing for her stall. Of course, she generally makes a lot of things herself, but with being ill she's not able to. Mrs. Porker went round to all the people while Miss Rossiter was ill, and told them to give all their things to her because Miss Rossiter wouldn't be having a stall, and they did. And now, of course, Miss Rossiter's well and going to have a stall, and there's *nothing* for it, and Mrs. Porker's delighted, because she *hates* her just because she used to own the Hall and knows everyone; and people have all given to Mrs. Porker and simply *won't* give again to Miss Rossiter, because you know getting anything out of people round here's like getting blood out of a stone—'

She paused for a long overdue breath, and William, looking at her fixedly, remarked:

'There isn't blood inside a stone.'

'I know,' said the visitor, 'that's the point.'

'Why did you say there was then?' said William.

'I didn't,' said the visitor. 'I said that getting anything out of people round here's like getting blood out of a stone.'

'But you can't get blood out of a stone,' said William.

'I know. That's what I meant.'

'Why did you say you could then?' said William.

'William,' said his mother, 'I think that it's your tea-time now.'

William swept up the final scrapings of cake-crumbs from his plate, put them into his mouth and made his way into the dining-room, where a solid tea, consisting of thick slices of bread and jam, awaited him. A grim-looking individual in black dress and apron (the Browns' long-suffering housemaid) was just setting a glass of milk at his place. William eyed the meal with disfavour, then uttered what was meant to represent an ironic laugh.

'No one ever thinks of givin' *me* anythin' decent to eat. I might die of starvation for anything any of you'd care.'

The housemaid looked him up and down.

'I've not seen many people looking less like dying of starvation than what you do,' was her comment.

'Oh, you think that, do you?' said William bitterly.

'Well, that's all you know about it. Let me tell you, people dyin' of starvation *don't* look thin. They sort of swell up, an' I bet that if I look fat that's why it is. I'm swelled up with starvation.'

He pointed scornfully to the plate of bread and jam. 'Expectin' anyone to *live* on that! Dry bread, same as what they give to people in dungeons!'

'It's not dry bread,' said the housemaid.

'It *is* dry bread,' said William, 'dry bread with a bit of jam on. That's all it is. What I say is, if the people in this house want to kill me, why don't they do it with a knife or a gun, 'stead of tryin' to starve me to death?'

But he was already attacking the plate of bread and jam with every appearance of relish, and the housemaid, muttering, 'You and your nonsense!' was preparing to leave the room when William called her back indistinctly through a mouthful of bread and jam.

'I say Ellen,' he said, 'there's a loony in the drawing-room with mother. She's escaped from an asylum.'

'Get out!' said Ellen, but lingered in the doorway for further details.

'Honest, she must have,' said William. 'She thinks that there's blood inside stones. She said so.'

'Go on! She never!' said Ellen, incredulous, but willing to be convinced.

'She did,' said William. 'She said so. I bet there's keepers lookin' for her somewhere this minute. I shouldn't be surprised if she's murdered mother by now, goin' vi'lent of a sudden like what they do. She said so. She said you'd find blood inside a stone if you cut it open.'

'Rubbish!' said Ellen, again preparing to leave the room.

'I say, Ellen,' said William. 'What do they have on fancy stalls?'

'Fancy things, of course,' said Ellen.

'What sort of fancy things?'

'Ornaments and handkerchiefs and—and pretty things.'

'You wouldn't do for one then, would you?' said William, with obvious delight at his own wit.

'I'd do a sight better than you,' retorted Ellen with spirit.

Then she went out of the room, but left the door open. William noticed with satisfaction that she stood for a second at the drawing-room door, gazing into it with fearful curiosity.

William proceeded to eat his bread and jam, but his mind was entirely taken up by the thought of Miss Rossiter and her fancy stall. Ornaments and handkerchiefs and pretty things. His eye roamed round the room. There

'EXPECTIN' ANYONE TO LIVE ON THAT!' SAID WILLIAM. 'DRY BREAD, SAME AS WHAT THEY GIVE TO PEOPLE IN DUNGEONS!'

were plenty of ornaments. He decided to take one secretly to Miss Rossiter every day for her fancy stall.

Pretty things. Ethel's room was full of things that people call pretty—powder bowls and dolls and cushions.

He'd take some of these along, too. And he'd just trust to his family's not missing them and not recognising them on the day of the bazaar. William was a very trustful boy. He felt elated at the thought of his undertaking. He'd show that old Mrs. Porker. He'd show her! If only he could survey her forces. How could he manage to enter the Hall unobserved, and see what Mrs. Porker had got for her stall, so as to be sure to outshine her? People, he ruminated, were always reading in the papers about robbers who got into houses by saying that they had come to look at the gas meter. He imagined himself going to the front door of the Hall and saying that he had come to look at the gas meter. He was trying hard to make this picture seem convincing (even with the false beard it somehow wasn't), when his mother entered with a note.

'Mrs. Meddows has just gone, dear,' she said, 'and I'd be so glad if you'd take a note to the Hall to Mrs. Porker. It's about the bazaar arrangements. Tell them that there's an answer.'

William walked up the long, winding drive and knocked on the front door. He knocked long and loudly because he was pretending that he was a detective going alone and unarmed to the house where the villain lived with his ill-gotten gains. He was going first to make the villain give him a written confession and then to summon his men and have him arrested. His men, of course, were hidden among the laurels in the shrubbery.

In the course of the struggle (previous to the writing of the confession), William and the villain would fall downstairs together, but fortunately William would be on the top. At this very moment, as his knocks echoed through the empty house, he pictured the villain crouching fearfully in a corner of the room in which the stolen treasure was hidden, listening . . .

William redoubled the violence of his knocks, imagining the cowering figure cowering back yet more fearfully, before 'with the courage born of despair,' as the last book he had read put it, he came down to face the avenger. The door opened suddenly. An indignant butler appeared, and William returned to real life.

'What's the matter with you?' said the butler angrily.

'Nothin',' retorted William. 'What's the matter with you?'

'Do you think we're all deaf?' proceeded the butler with displeasure.

'I dunno what you are,' said William. 'You look as if you might be anything.'

'What have you come for?' said the butler, deciding to cease his attempts at repressing the irrespressible.

'Gotter note for Mrs. Porker,' said William; 'an' it wants an answer.'

He was entering jauntily, when the butler put out a large hand to push him back.

'I'll take the note,' he said with majestic aloofness. 'You stay out there.'

'Huh!' said William darkly, returning to his character of a famous detective. 'You'd better be careful what you do to *me*. You'd be jolly surprised if you knew who I was. I've gotter right to go into any house I like, I have.'

At this point a very stout woman, dressed in black and freely ornamented with pearls and diamonds, appeared in the hall, and said:

'What's the matter, Jenkins?'

Jenkins turned his majestic countenance towards her, and said in a voice expressive of patient suffering:

'It's a boy, madam, with a note. He was insisting on coming into the house.'

'Well, why shouldn't he,' said the lady, 'if he's got a note?'

'Look at his boots, madam,' said Jenkins in a tone of still deeper suffering.

'Well, you can sweep up a bit of mud, can't you?' said the lady tartly. 'What d'you think you're paid for?'

Jenkins turned on her a look before which a duchess

'IT' S A BOY, MADAM, WITH A NOTE,' SAID JENKINS, 'HE WAS INSISTING ON COMING INTO THE HOUSE.'

had quailed, but the lady's protective armour of pearls and diamonds merely shot back defiance, so he turned to vanish slowly through a green baize door, his dignity unimpaired.

'Thinks he can come it over me,' muttered the lady angrily, ' 'Im an' 'is dukes!'

Then she swept William into a small morning-room, and said:

'Sit down, or 'ave a look round just as you like,' and she sat down herself to answer his mother's letter.

William had a look round. He found a Chinese mandarin that he could set nodding, an ivory elephant that he could balance on top of a clock, and a pair of silver nutcrackers. He experimented with these by cracking a small piece of coal surreptitiously abstracted from the coal box. This last attracted the lady's attention.

''Ere,' she said, 'stop muckin' about like that.'

Impressed by her tone and vocabulary, William stopped mucking about like that, and sat down on a small sofa, where he contented himself with drawing out strands of fringe that edged a cushion and absent-mindedly eating them.

Finally the lady turned round.

'Well, I've wrote to your ma,' she said, 'tellin' 'er all about where 'er stall's to be an' refreshments an' so on. Now you come with me an' 'ave a look at the things I've got for *my* stall. Make 'em all sit up, they will.'

She led William upstairs to a room that was literally knee deep in fancy articles. Cushions, mats, dolls, fans, fancy handkerchiefs, nightdress-cases, handkerchief-cases and lace-trimmed underclothing, lay massed in heaps everywhere. William gazed about him in dismay.

'Crumbs!' he gasped.

'*There!*' said the lady proudly. '*That's* going to be a stall an' a half, ain't it?'

'Yes,' said William, 'but—but,' he went on with exaggerated innocence, 'but I think there's too much an' it'll spoil it. I'd give some of these things to the other person.'

'What other person?'

'Well,' said William, trying to be very diplomatic, 'isn't there someone else havin' a fancy stall?'

For he had realised that the entire 'fancy' element of his home, brought bit by bit, and day by day to Miss Rossiter's, would have no chance against this collection.

''Er!' spat out Mrs. Porker viciously, and her large face purpled angrily. ''Er! That Rossiter woman! Why d'you think I've slaved myself to skin an' bone'—William shot a fascinated glance at her ample proportions—'over this 'ere stall? To show 'er up, that's why! She's 'ardly got six penn'orth of stuff, she 'asn't, an' she won't 'ave neither. Look small, beside all this, won't she—'er an' her pedigree tree!'

'It's a beech tree,' said William. 'It just meets the other, but you can't get across.'

But Mrs. Porker wasn't listening.

'Look at me,' she continued dramatically, 'an' tell me if there's any reason why the swells shouldn't call on me same as they used to on 'er.'

William looked at her. He felt vaguely that there was some reason, but he felt, too, that it would be difficult as well as indiscreet to express it in words.

'Why don't they call?' went on his hostess explosively. 'I'll tell you why they don't. 'Cause of 'er an' 'er champagne of calamity!'

'Her what?' said William, interested.

'Well, say it yourself if you can say it any better,' said the lady with spirit. 'I seed it in a book, so it must be all right.' Then her indignation suddenly left her, and she gazed mournfully about her. 'Though it's 'ard to put any 'eart into anything now with my little Pongo— Did you know my little Pongo?'

William fixed her with a blank look. There had been an occasion not very long ago when Mrs. Porker had narrowly rescued Pongo from the jaws of death in the person of Jumble. But, though William had cheered Jumble on to the deed, he had remained in the background, and it was evident that the lady did not connect him with the incident.

'Pongo?' he said with an air of imbecility meant to express innocence.

'My dear, dear little four-footed friend,' said Mrs. Porker, wiping away a tear; ' 'e crossed over last week.'

'Crossed over?' said William. 'What was he? Oxford.'

'What d'you mean?' said Mrs. Porker indignantly.

'You said he'd crossed over,' said William. 'I thought you meant from Oxford to Cambridge or from Lib'ral to Conservative, or something like that.'

'I meant 'e died, of course,' said Mrs. Porker irritably, then returned to her lamentations.

'I *knew* there was bad luck about all last week. I'm not superstitious, but I do believe in bad luck. I went under a ladder on Monday, an' on Tuesday I saw two magpies, an' Wednesday I 'eard an owl moanin' all night, an' on Thursday I met that there Miss Rossiter, an' she can smile, but she can't 'ide from me that she's got the hevil eye. She ill-wished my poor little Pongo and that's wot did for 'im. Come an' look at my poor little Pongo's kennel.'

William followed her out into the garden. There was a wooden erection, made in the shape of a doll's house, with little windows and curtains and a large front door.

'The door 'ad to be made larger once or twice as 'e got stouter,' said Pongo's mistress tearfully. ''E was a good eater for his size an' 'e'd stoutened up considerably, lately. I come 'ere to 'is little kennel,' she went on, 'every night, I do, so's to let 'im know I've not forgotten 'im.'

'Thought you said he was dead,' said William.

'Well, 'is *spirit* isn't dead, is it?' said Mrs. Porker tartly. ''E's got a spirit, 'asn't 'e?'

''As 'e?' said William absently.

'Yes an'—well now, a friend of mine told me that someone that a friend of a friend of hers knows lost a dog, an' every night after that she used to go down to his empty kennel—'

'Why didn't she go to the police to see if they could find it?'

'It was *dead*, I tell you,' said Mrs. Porker, annoyed at having her story interrupted. 'You don't seem to have any *sense*. Well, every night she used to go down to his kennel and she used to hear his little bark comin' from far away like a little spirit bark. An' it used to sort of tell 'er what to do. She used to sort of listen an' its bark sounded like 'Don't' or 'Do' to the thing she was thinking of doing.

'An' if it seemed to say "Don't" she knew there was bad luck about it an' she wouldn't do it, an' if it seemed to say "Do" she'd know there was good luck about an' she'd do it. It was its little spirit barkin' its message to her. Some people said that it was a dog down the road she used to 'ear, but some people are always ready to say nasty things like that.

'An' that's why I come down 'ere every night to listen for my little Pongo's message—my poor little Pongo what was ill-wished by that witch, an' pined away. An' *that's* why I've got to 'ave a slap up fancy stall to show 'ers up. It's not much to do to avenge my poor little Pongo, but it's something.'

William was walking home. He was both interested and bewildered. He felt as if the situation were a puzzle that would be quite easy to solve if only he had a key. Then he forgot all about it, and spent an interesting hour trying to teach Jumble to be a water spaniel. William found Jumble far more interesting than he would have found a dog of a definite breed. There were so many sorts of dogs that Jumble might be but wasn't, that he led a more varied existence than on the whole he liked. He had had extensive courses of training as a sheep dog and as a blood-hound and he thought that he preferred either of them to the water spaniel training. He adored William, however, and he was a philosophical sort of a dog, who realised that everything came to an end, and that sooner or later William would have to go home to supper.

He was walking now at William's heels, still dripping with water, but pirouetting happily about, because he knew that William would have completely forgotten about his being a water spaniel by the time he'd finished his supper. As a matter of fact, William was already an explorer in a hitherto unexplored country and Jumble (although he didn't know it) was a train of mules and camels carrying his provisions and ammunition.

Every now and then William would stop and, shading his eyes with his hand, would gaze slowly around him, feeling vaguely annoyed with the roofs and chimneys that insisted on meeting his view.

Suddenly in the garden of a cottage that he was passing (he was pretending that it was a hill infested with man-eating tigers, and he was keeping an imaginary gun trained upon it) he spied a dog sitting motionless on a chair just outside the door. William forgot that he was an explorer and hung over the gate uttering his most provocative growl. William was proud of his growl. It could goad most dogs to fury in a few seconds. But the dog remained unmoved, remained, in fact, staring in front of it with glassy eyes as if it didn't see or hear him.

William was just going on in disgust when he saw that Jumble had wormed himself through a hole in the hedge and was springing upon the creature with every appearance of hostility. The creature fell to the ground and there Jumble flung himself upon it again with redoubled efforts.

William saw to his horror that the creature was a stuffed dog and that it was in danger of being completely disintegrated by Jumble's spirited onset. William knew by experience that he would be held responsible for the destruction. Horrible visions of weeks without pocket-money flashed before his eyes, and, forgetful of everything else, he flung open the gate and hurled himself upon the unequal battle.

'Drop it! Let go, you old fool! Get off it!' he shouted authoritatively to Jumble. A little old man appeared at the cottage door just as William was throwing Jumble clear of his unresisting victim. Jumble, aware that he had incurred his master's displeasure and anxious to avoid the consequences, took to his heels and flew like an arrow down the road.

William and the little old man stood at the gate and watched him. Right in the distance could be seen the figure of a middle-aged lady. Jumble had just reached the figure as it turned the bend of the road.

'*Well*,' said the old man as they disappeared from view, 'wouldn't you think shed've stopped to see what 'er dawg were a'doin' of? Some folks don't know how to keep a dawg in order. Goin' on like that an' lettin' it stay be'ind to worrit my poor Toby. If I knew 'oo she was I'd make 'er pay, I would.'

William, much relieved at the turn of events had taken, emitted a vague murmur of sympathy and assent, and hoped that Jumble would not be so rash as to return before he had made his escape. The little old man was picking up the overthrown Toby and examining him carefully.

''E won't stand much knockin' abaht,' he was saying

anxiously. ''E got the moth in 'im last year an' 'e's gotter be treated careful. That's why I put im out 'ere in the sunshine to try'n' get 'im free of moth. My pal 'e 'is. 'Im an' me used to do a turn what was known in every 'all through England.'

'What sort of a turn?' said William.

'Ventriloquist turn, of course,' said the old man scornfully. 'Never 'eard of Nelson an' 'is dawg Toby? That were me. Why, I can 'ear 'em clappin' now!' He sat down on the chair with the stuffed dog on his knee and said: 'Now, Toby, tell me where you were last night.' And the dog without a second's hesitation answered in a series of yaps: 'Mind your own business.'

William stood there spellbound, his eyes and mouth wide open. For the yaps were the same short, shrill yaps as Mrs. Porker's late lamented little dog Pongo used to utter.

'It's—dead, isn't it?' said William, approaching the stuffed dog fearfully.

'Oh, yes,' laughed the old man. 'It's *me* doin' it really. I'm a bit rusty, but you never forgets a thing like that. Not to say *forget*. Just a trick of the throat you know.'

He was evidently flattered by William's admiration and surprise.

He turned to the little dog again, and carried on a further conversation with it. The back chat of which it was composed was somewhat primitive, but the yapping replies were the most wonderful thing that William had ever heard in his life.

''E'd've been tore up past mendin' if you'd not come in an' sent that ole woman's dawg off, an' I'm grateful to you, young sir. An' if there's anythin' I can ever do for you, you jus' let me know an' I'll do it.'

William stood staring in front of him like one entranced. He saw himself in Miss Rossiter's garden and he heard Miss Rossiter telling him about her stall at the bazaar; he saw himself in Mrs. Porker's garden standing by Pongo's kennel; he heard Mrs. Porker saying: 'I come down 'ere every night to listen for my little Pongo's message.'

He'd found the key to the puzzle.

He turned to the man and said in a hoarse earnest voice:

'There *is* somethin' you could do for me if—if—if you'd do it.' And he told the old man what was in his mind.

The next evening Pongo's elaborate kennel stood outlined in the gathering dusk as his mistress came through the garden. She halted in front of it, her large face wearing an expression of ludicrously exaggerated grief, and said: 'Pongo, my poor dear little Pongo, are you 'appy, Pongo?'

It was obvious from her voice that she wasn't expecting

an answer, but there came an answer—a sharp, short yap—querulous, peevish, and threatening, Pongo's very own. It came unmistakably from the empty kennel.

Had not the elaborate coiffeur upon Mrs. Porker's head been of alien growth, it would assuredly have stood on end. Her eyes bulged out so far that William, hidden in the bushes with Toby's master, thought for one thrilling moment that they were going to fall on to the ground. Her mouth opened and shut like that of an expiring fish.

'Oh, Pongo!' she said at last, clasping her fat little hands, 'Pongo, is it really you?'

Again the yap answered her from the empty kennel.

'Oh, Pongo!' panted Mrs. Porker, her eyes still as round as marbles, 'oh, Pongo, 'ave you any message for me?'

Again the answer came from the empty kennel in a series of yaps that were still quite plainly words.

'There's — bad — luck — about — those — things — you've — got — for — your — stall. Give — them — to — her — what — ill-wished — me.'

'Oh, Pongo!' said Mrs. Porker tearfully. 'Oh, I will! Oh! Pongo—do tell me. Pongo, do they look after you all right where you've gone? Do they see your chicken's tender?'

But there came no answer, and soon Mrs. Porker, moaning hysterically, tottering unsteadily upon her high heels, returned to the house.

William and the little old man crept cautiously out of the bushes and back to the road. There the old man stood, drew a deep breath, and mopped his brow.

'I din't like a-doin' of it,' he said; 'but a promise is a promise.'

'It was jolly decent of you,' said William gratefully. 'I'll make you a whistle. I can. A man showed me how to. It whistles, too. Not loud, but it whistles.'

'Thank you,' said the old man without enthusiasm. 'Well, I'll be gettin' home.'

At that moment Jumble came up and was on the point of greeting William tumultuously when William said hastily: 'That's that dog. It must've got lost. I'll take it back to its home,' and seized the surprised Jumble by the collar, and holding him low on the ground in order to make his progress appear reluctant, began to pull him homewards.

The old man stood watching them and scratching his head thoughtfully.

Miss Rossiter's stall was the sensation of the bazaar. Never had such a prolific display of expensive fancy goods been seen on a stall before. Large crowds surrounded it during the whole afternoon. Occasionally Miss Rossiter would explain in a bewildered fashion:

'Mrs. Porker sent them to me. It was so *kind* of her. She said that she'd got enough for herself without.'

Mrs. Porker at another fancy stall, that had been very inadequately stocked at the last minute, gazed across with horrified fascination at Miss Rossiter, expecting every moment some terrible calamity would befall her.

As the afternoon wore on and nothing happened to Miss Rossiter, except universal congratulations and enormous sales, she began to look rather puzzled.

William had attached himself to Miss Rossiter for the afternoon and was busying himself 'helping' at her stall. He sold a pile of things that had been already sold and put aside for their owners. He sold Miss Rossiter's parasol and scarf. He gave wrong change on a generous scale. He told Sir Charles Politt, who had opened the bazaar, to clear off and stop taking up all the room if he wasn't going to buy anything. In short, he worked very hard all the afternoon.

After the bazaar was over he helped Miss Rossiter to carry her belongings home.

'Thank you so much, dear,' she said as she regaled him with iced buns in her little dining-room. 'You've been such a help. Isn't it wonderful how everything's turned out? Do you remember how I told you all my troubles that day you fell down from my beech tree? I was so afraid that my little stall would be a failure. And it's been the most tremendous success. All owing to the kindness of Mrs. Porker. I feel *so* grateful to her.'

At that minute Mrs. Porker burst into the room.

'Oh, Miss Rossiter,' she began, wringing her hands, ''*as* anything 'appened to you?'

'To me?' said Miss Rossiter, surprised. 'No.'

'No ill luck of no kind?' said Mrs. Porker anxiously.

'No,' said Miss Rossiter. 'Quite the contrary.'

'I'd never 'ave forgiven myself if it 'ad,' said Mrs. Porker. 'Let's 'ope the bad luck got scattered to the wind when the things come out into the open air like.'

Miss Rossiter gazed at her in blank amazement, but Mrs. Porker continued tremulously:

'I see I was wrong an' poor dear Pongo was wrong, but it was my fault 'e was wrong 'cause I'd told 'im you'd ill-wished 'im an' the poor little chap believed it. I saw I was wrong this afternoon when they was all so kind to me, an' Sir Charles 'imself sayin' as 'ow you'd asked 'im to call an' 'e'd been too busy but 'oped to come next week, an' I thought then that if anythin'd 'appened to you with me sending you them things I'd never forgive myself.'

'Mrs. Porker,' said Miss Rossiter, in a kind but bewildered voice, 'you—you seem overwrought. It must be the heat. Just sit down there while I get you a cup of tea.'

Mrs. Porker flopped down heavily on to a chair.

'Well, I *would* like a cup of tea, dearie,' she admitted.

William slipped quietly from the room and set off homewards down the road.

It was supper time and he didn't want to be late. Though he'd had an excellent tea at the bazaar and he'd just had four iced buns at Miss Rossiter's, he was still hungry and didn't want to miss supper.

He felt no elation at the success of his little plot. He'd merely wiped off a feeling of indebtedness to Miss Rossiter.

As he walked down the road gazing about him with stern frowning brows, he wasn't thinking of the events of the last few days at all. He was a lion roaming through the jungle in search of prey. Jumble, trotting happily by his side, was his faithful lioness.

CHAPTER 10

# WILLIAM AND THE TWINS

Honeysuckle Cottage stood empty and William (who always took a great interest in Honeysuckle Cottage) made a short detour on his way to school every morning in order to pass it, and see if there were yet any signs of new artist inhabitants.

His joy therefore was great one morning when, on his way to school, he saw unmistakable signs of occupation, all the windows open and an easel standing in the little garden. An Artist. William, who had long experience of the Arts, as temporarily domiciled in Honeysuckle Cottage, was glad that the new-comer was an artist. He always found artists were more interesting and better-tempered than writers. And, of course, their paints and palettes, when left unguarded, were fascinating things to experiment with.

He was so taken up with the thoughts of the new arrivals that he got all his sums wrong and had to stay in, and that left him no time for further exploring that evening.

He was up early next morning, however, and made his way at once to Honeysuckle Cottage. He crept cautiously up the path and peered in at the open kitchen door. And there he stood motionless. For a most extraordinary couple were engaged upon preparations for breakfast. Both had exactly the same faces—long and pale and narrow, framed in short lank fair hair. Both wore white silk shirts and coats of home spun tweeds. That one was a man and the other a woman was evident from the fact that one wore knickerbockers and the other a skirt, but the fact that both garments were of exactly the same length made the effects remarkably similar. Beneath these garments, they wore worsted stockings and brogues. Both were leaning over the gas stove, the man anxiously watching a saucepan of eggs, the woman making coffee. The woman turned round suddenly, and saw William standing in the open doorway.

'Watch this and see that it doesn't boil,' she said to him casually, 'or else take those plates into the dining-room.'

'I'll take the plates,' said William, thrilled to the very core at being thus accepted as a member of the party. He carried the plates into the dining-room, put them on to the little gate-legged table, and returned to the kitchen.

'These eggs are done, I should think,' the man remarked to him as soon as he entered. 'Do you know how to get them out of the boiling water?'

William and the man had a very interesting time getting them out of the boiling water (there were six of them) and then they carried them into the dining-room on a plate. There the man looked at them with rather a worried frown.

'Have I done too many?' he said. 'I just put in all the man brought.'

'Oh no,' said William reassuringly. 'I don't think they're too many.'

The man seemed cheered.

'No, I suppose there aren't.'

The woman had just come in with the coffee and he pointed to her, to William, and to himself. 'No, of course, just two each, isn't it? That's not too many.'

William sat down with prompt obedience on one of the three chairs that the man placed at the table. The woman passed him a cup of coffee, the man gave him two eggs and the meal began. The man and the woman talked animatedly, but William was too much thrilled to speak, and certainly too thrilled to listen. The strange couple accepted him without question, as evidently they would have accepted without question anyone who appeared. There was a loaf of bread and a plate of butter, to which William helped himself liberally.

Suddenly the woman looked at him and said: 'Why

aren't you drinking your coffee?'

'I never drink coffee,' said William. 'I don't like it.'

She looked at the man and sighed.

'He's right, you know,' she said. 'One shouldn't drink stimulants of any sort if one wants to keep the psychic faculties unclouded. He's quite right.' She turned to William again. 'What do you drink?'

'I drink liqu'rice water mostly,' said William.

'Liquorice water,' she said vaguely. 'I must try it.'

Then she began to talk to the man again. William, who had finished his eggs and a large part of the bread and butter, murmured something about going home to breakfast, but neither of them took any notice of him. So he departed quietly homeward, where he made an excellent breakfast of porridge, scrambled eggs, toast, butter, and marmalade.

Rather to his surprise, he was not kept in that day (William was kept in so regularly that, when he wasn't, he always felt as if he'd been let out an hour earlier than the right time), and he made his way at once to Honeysuckle Cottage. The man was seated at an easel in the little orchard, and the woman was in the kitchen, just putting on the kettle. Dishes, crockery, utensils of every sort, lay on table and chairs, and even on the floor. Never before had William seen a kitchen in such a state of disorder, and his heart warmed to it. It was, he felt, a kitchen that he would like to live in. Absent-mindedly he began to eat sultanas from an open canister that was perched precariously upon the soap dish. The woman turned to him, and again accepted his presence unquestioningly.

'Have we enough things for tea,' she said, 'or shall we have to wash some?'

They began to hunt among the crockery for cups and plates. William found two clean cups and his hostess washed a third in a primitive fashion under the tap. Then she seemed to forget about the tea, and wandered vaguely out into the garden. William accompanied her. She sat down on a deck-chair on the little lawn and William sat at her feet. Suddenly she looked at William and said: 'Do you see nature spirits?'

William stared at her in amazement.

'Perhaps you know them better as fairies,' she said. 'Do you ever see fairies?'

'Do I—?' repeated William, and his voice died away in horror . . .

'Children,' went on the lady, apparently unaware of the monstrous insult she had just offered him, 'children often do see them, though my great friend Elissa Freedom—you may have heard of her, she's well known in the psychic world—says that she didn't see them as a child, though she sees them now quite plainly. I really must show you some of her photographs. They're most interesting. Not small, like the conventional nature spirit, though there *are* those, too, I'm sure. She has a lovely one of a birch tree with the outline of a nature spirit standing near it. About the size of a child . . . faint, you know, but quite unmistakable. She says that everything in nature has its attendant spirit. Of the same colour generally. Even,' she gazed around the little garden, then pointed to the heap of grass cuttings that stood by the greenhouse, 'even that heap of grass cuttings has its attendant spirit. Green, nebulous, unmistakable. My friend Elissa would probably see it as she sat here with us. I wish you could see her photographs. I've brought a camera with me, but so far I haven't had any success.'

'Uh-huh,' agreed William, completely mystified.

'That of course, is why Tristram and I have come here,' she went on. 'Tristram is my twin brother. You know him, of course?'

'Oh yes,' said William. 'I know him.'

After all he'd had breakfast with him only that morning.

'We want to cultivate our psychic faculties. My brother will—er—surrender himself to psychic influences in the hope of doing inspirational painting, and I am going to try to cultivate my psychic vision till I can see a nature spirit. All the authorities say that to retire into the country is the best way to cultivate the psychic faculties. That, of course, is why we have come here. I take it that you are interested in the psychic side of life?'

'Uh-huh,' agreed William again.

He hadn't the remotest conception what the psychic side of life was, but he was quite ready to be interested in whatever the lady was interested in. She was unlike anyone else he had ever met, and William always liked people who were unlike anyone else he had ever met.

'Have you ever had any experiences?'

'Me?' said William. 'Oh yes, lots.'

But before he could tell her any of his favourite imaginary exploits (she'd have been disappointed because, though thrilling and blood curdling enough for anyone, there was nothing psychic about them) the church clock struck five, and she rose slowly from her deck chair.

'It's tea time, I suppose,' she said. 'I don't remember whether I put the kettle on or not. Do you?'

William said that she had, and they went in to find the kitchen floor a swamp of boiling water. The lady contemplated the phenomenon with mild interest.

'I suppose it must have boiled over,' she said. 'It's funny how they do that, isn't it? I know there's a reason, but I've never really understood it. I suppose it'll dry all right, if we leave it, won't it? Let's find some plates and things now.'

It was delicious sloshing about the water-logged kitchen floor. William surreptitiously poured a little more on it from the kettle to make it yet more enjoyable. He jumped in it, and trailed round, dragging his feet. He splashed it up with first one foot and then the other, and sailed a little cream carton (which he found in the blacking box) in it, making magnificent waves and finally wrecking it against the feet of the gas stove. Meantime the lady, who did not seem to mind his doing this in the least, was vaguely searching for clean crockery among the stacks of clean and dirty crockery that stood indiscriminately everywhere. When she found some she carried it into the little dining-room. Finally she examined the kettle.

'There isn't enough left to make tea,' she said, 'and, of course, one really shouldn't drink stimulants when one's trying to acquire psychic vision.' She turned suddenly to William. 'What did you say you drank?'

'Me?' said William. 'Liqu'rice water mostly.'

'Liquorice water? I don't think I've ever tasted it. Where do you get it? Would the Stores supply it?'

'I make it,' said William modestly.

He pulled a bottle out of his pocket and with an air of great gallantry poused some into a saucer for her to drink. She tasted it with a critical frown. The critical frown vanished.

'It's very nice,' she said. 'A pure herbal drink, of course.'

'Uh-huh!' said William, who hadn't the remotest idea what herbal meant.

'You must show me how to make it,' she said.

'I'll make you some,' said William. 'Give me twopence, an' I'll run 'n' get some liqu'rice from the shop.'

She gave him sixpence, because, as she said, one might as well have a good supply, and, very importantly, William made a jug of liquorice water in the kitchen. He was more thrilled by this than by anything else that happened in this fascinating household. He'd never before met a grown-up who did not look upon liquorice water as a messy juvenile concoction to be thrown away with contumacy whenever discovered.

Tea was ready at last, and Tristram came in from his easel in the orchard. His sister poured him out a cup of the liquorice water.

'I thought, Tristram,' she said, 'that during this retirement from the world we should give up stimulants. They dull the psychic faculties, you know, so we're having liquorice water. Taste it and see if you like it.'

Tristram tasted it.

'Delicious,' he said, 'quite delicious.'

'The boy made it,' said his sister, 'but I daresay the Stores could get it for us. The boy always drinks liquorice water and he says that he has had psychic experiences.'

William, who had come to the conclusion that 'psychic' was a synonym for 'exciting,' swallowed a large piece of bread and butter in order to embark upon some of his imaginary exploits against Red Indians, and world famous gangs of criminals, but Tristram was delivering a monologue full of incomprehensible art terms.

'Have you had any success?' said his sister when he stopped for breath.

'N-not exactly,' he confessed. 'I—I surrender myself and try to paint what comes into my head, as it were, but I can't help realising that it isn't as good as the work in which I *don't* surrender myself.'

William, going into the kitchen after tea, was horrified to find a woman from the village there, mopping up the kitchen floor and glaring at the chaos around her.

'You get out of here,' she said sharply to William, seeing in him instinctively an enemy of law and order.

The lady appeared in the doorway.

'Oh, you've come,' she said vaguely, 'they said at the Post Office they'd find someone.'

'Yes, they found me,' said the woman grimly, 'and a nice state the place is in!'

‘IT’ S VERY NICE,’ SHE SAID. ‘A PURE HERBAL DRINK, OF COURSE.’

The lady looked round it with quite amiable interest.

'Yes, I suppose it is,' she said vaguely, 'I really hadn't thought of it.'

The fascination of the inside of the cottage had completely disappeared for William with the advent of the 'woman,' but the outside remained. The activities of the sister (whose name, William had discovered, was Miss Auriole Mannister) were not very exciting. She sat gazing wistfully about the little garden, her camera posed for action upon whatever nature spirit should appear to her. She asked William to leave the garden undisturbed to her between four and five o'clock, explaining that she was concentrating on that hour, because she thought that her psychic functions were most active then. She asked him diffidently, and as if he had quite as much business there as she had. It never seemed to occur to her or to her brother to wonder where he came from, or to question his right of entry to either cottage or garden. William was very careful to absent himself from the garden from four to five, the more so as he was finding the artist in the orchard even more interesting than the vision-seeker in the garden. The artist sat before his easel with a palette in his hand and a large box of paints by his side, executing on his canvas a series of amazing strokes that were evidently meant to represent the orchard, but that reminded William of the nightmare he had had after last year's November the fifth's firework display. The artist noticed the expression with which William was watching it and said in his gentle melancholy voice:

'It's not meant to represent what one sees, you know. It's meant to represent the emotions the sight of it rouses in one.'

'Yes,' said William, trying to sound as if he understood.

The thrill of watching these displays gradually wore off, of course, and yet something about them was vaguely inspiring. William had always considered that he could paint as well as anyone but he hadn't realised that painting pictures—real pictures—was *quite* as easy as that, simply splodging paint about anyhow. It simplified the art considerably. William felt inspired to make attempts himself. He surreptitiously tore pages out of his exercise books at school, and took them to the cottage with him. There, furtively and under cover of examining the paint boxes, he 'borrowed' paint very cautiously, till he found that the artist took the situation as a matter of course. If William happened to be using the paint tube he wanted, he would wait quite patiently till William had finished with it. If William put it down on the wrong side of his chair, he would ask for it very politely.

Gradually William came to look upon himself as a finished artist. Certainly he considered that his pictures were just as good as Tristram's, except that perhaps they were a little more like the object he was copying. He boasted of his skill to his friends till Ginger, nettled by his boastful claims, said: 'All right, draw us something then an' let's see.'

'All right, I will,' said William. 'I jolly well will. What'll I draw you?'

'Draw us a sign to put up at the ole barn.'

'All right. What'll I paint on it?'

'A lion.'

'All right. I'll do it to-night an' I'll show it to you to-morrow an' then you'll jolly well *see!*'

So William began his lion that evening. The artist was working indoors in water colours and he had prepared some large white squares to paint upon. They were quite a nice size for a sign for the old barn. Seeing William furtively reaching out a hand to abstract one, the man passed him one absently and both of them set to work. Once Miss Auriole looked in and whispered: 'How are you getting on, Tristram?' and Tristram said: 'I'm surrendering myself *utterly*, but I don't know what the results will be.'

'I *do* hope it will be all right,' said his sister rather doubtfully, and added: 'I'm waiting and watching with my camera outside.'

William finished his lion before he went home to bed. He considered it an excellent lion. It looked as spirited and wild and ferocious as a lion ought to look and seldom does. When he had finished it, he went out to look at Miss Auriole. She was asleep in a deckchair in the orchard with her camera on her knee.

Then he went home to tea and didn't realise till he was in bed that he'd left his lion behind in the little studio.

He explained to Ginger the next morning.

'I've done it an' it's a *jolly* good lion.'

'Where is it?'

'I've not got it. I forget an' left it there.'

'Oh, yes!' jeered Ginger.

'Well, you come round with me after school an' jolly well *see!*'

'All right,' said Ginger, 'I'll b'lieve when I see it.'

'Yes, I bet you will too.'

After school William took Ginger round to the cottage. They entered the garden cautiously. William had not before taken any of his friends to the cottage. He had felt a sort of responsibility towards this trusting couple, and had shielded them, as far as possible, from boys in the plural. Ginger looked about the garden with interest.

'A jolly good place for Hide and Seek,' he said.

William was creeping towards the study window.

'My paintin's in here,' he said, then he stopped.

Through the study window he could see his two friends and a strange man with a beard standing round the little desk. He retreated.

'We'll wait till they come out,' he said.

'Let's have a game of Hide and Seek,' said Ginger.

'All right. I'll hide. You count.'

'One . . . two . . . three . . .'

William crept down to the bottom of the lawn where the heap of grass cutting stood, and with a dexterous movement inserted himself into the very middle of it. Soon he heard Ginger shout 'Com—' and stop suddenly. Then he heard the sounds of the lady setting up her deck-chair on the lawn. Ginger had evidently vanished abruptly on sight of her. William remained in his grass heap wondering what to do. It was the hour during which the lady had asked him to leave her undisturbed. William felt reluctant to intrude upon it. She had, he felt, treated him with such consideration that she deserved consideration in return. For a moment he meditated remaining where he was till the end of the hour. But he was already tired of swallowing grass cuttings and he didn't like the taste of them. Then the memory of the lady, fast asleep in the deck-chair the day before, returned to him. If he waited just a few minutes, it would be all right. She'd be fast asleep. He waited till he imagined that he heard deep breathing, then rose from the heap, fled behind the greenhouse and out through a hole in the hedge. Simultaneous sounds of a gasp and a click pursued him. Scattering grass cuttings at every step he hastened down to the road. There he met his mother. She gazed at him in horrified amazement.

'*William!* What have you been doing?'

'Me?' said William in innocent surprise. 'Nothin'. Why?'

'You're *covered* with grass.'

'Oh that,' said William casually. 'Oh, I dunno. I s'pose I sat down in a field or somethin'.'

'What nonsense! Come home with me at once.'

Despite his protests, she took him home and brushed him and washed him till there was not an atom of grass left on him. Feeling depressed by this process, he set out again to find Ginger. He found him hanging about the gate of the cottage.

'Hello!' he greeted William. 'I've been lookin' all over

for you. I had to go 'cause she came out. Where were you hidin'?'

'In the grass.'

'Well, let's try'n' get your paintin' now.'

They entered the little garden again.

Tristram was just joining his sister on the lawn.

'Tristram!' she greeted him excitedly, 'I've seen one. Oh, my dear! It was so thrilling. I was sitting here as usual with my camera, watching and waiting, when suddenly from that grass heap there detached itself a faint green wraith—a shadowy spirit. For one second I saw it standing by the heap as plainly as I see you now, and then it disappeared.'

'You got a snap of it, I hope,' said Tristram anxiously.

'Yes, my dear. Oh, I hope so. If what I saw comes out, I can die happy. And what about yours, my dear?'

Tristram's face clouded over.

'It's no good. Tosher says that none of them will do for the journal. He says that they aren't *inspirational enough*.'

'Oh, *Tristram!* I'm so sorry.'

'It is a great disappointment, I won't deny it,' said Tristram, his long melancholy face more melancholy than ever. 'I'd so completely surrendered myself to influence.'

'Oh, dear, I *am* sorry . . . where is he? Has he gone?'

'No, he's still in the study. His train doesn't go till half-past.'

'Let's go out for a walk, dear. It will do you good. He won't mind being left till his train goes, I'm sure.'

Together the twins set off for their walk.

Ginger and William crept round to the little studio, but the man with the beard was still there.

'I can't get it now,' said William.

'I don't b'lieve you ever did it,' said Ginger.

'All right,' said William, 'you wait till to-morrow when I can go in an' get it an' *then* you'll talk a bit diff'rent.'

To-morrow came and William went into the little studio, but he couldn't find his lion painting. He hunted the studio without success. Ginger spent a pleasant day jeering at him, till William, stung to retaliation, wrung a recantation out of him with his head in the ditch.

After that they both completely forgot the incident.

There were all the signs of departure at Honeysuckle Cottage. Boxes stood packed on the doorstep. The decrepit village cab was at the little gate. William hung about disconsolately. He had spent many enjoyable hours in the little cottage, and he was sorry to say good-bye to his friends. He was making himself useful to the best of his ability. He had already carried down an unpacked suit-case and had to take it back again, and he had packed several 'fixtures' of the cottage that had necessitated the boxes being unpacked again to the bottom. Suddenly he saw the postman at the gate and went down to get the letters.

There were two bulky packets of papers—one for Tristram and one for his sister. The sister fell upon hers with a cry of joy, and unwrapped half a dozen papers bearing the inscription 'Psychic Realms.'

'My photograph!' she said, turning over the pages with trembling fingers.

Then she gave a scream of excitement.

'Here it is! Look!'

William and Tristram looked. There was a photograph of the grass heap at the end of the lawn, and by it the grass-covered figure of William, preparing to creep furtively away. Beneath it was the legend, 'Nature Spirit, photographed by Miss Auriole Mannister.'

William gaped at it, speechless with amazement, his eyes and mouth wide open.

Before he could say anything, however, Tristram, too, had uttered a cry of surprise and excitement. He too had unwrapped half a dozen copies of the 'Psychic Realm' and had a letter in his hand.

'Listen,' he said, 'it's from Tosher. He says "After you'd

MISS AURIOLE GAVE A SCREAM OF EXCITEMENT.
‘HERE IT IS! LOOK!’ SHE EXCLAIMED.

gone I found a really splendid bit of inspirational painting in your studio. Why didn’t you show it to me? It’s truly inspired. I have called it ‘Vision,’ and it’s reproduced on page twenty-six.”’

Both of them turned over the pages frenziedly.

‘Here it is. Look?’

And there was William's lion and underneath the words, 'Vision. Inspiration painting, by Mr. Tristram Mannister.'

'But, do you know,' said Tristram in an awestruck voice, 'I haven't the slightest memory of ever doing it.'

'You must have done it in a state of ecstasy, dear,' said Miss Auriole reverently.

'I must,' said Tristram. 'It's—it's the most wonderful thing that's ever happened to me.'

Then the cabman called to them from his perch saying that, blimey, they'd miss it if they didn't hurry, and they had gone before William recovered the power of speech.

They had, however, left a copy of the 'Psychic Realm' behind them, and William, with mingled feelings of pride and bewilderment, picked it up and put it in his pocket.

He showed the two pictures to everyone he knew, pointing out that the nature spirit was himself, and that he had executed the inspirational painting of 'Vision.' No one, of course, believed him.

THE END

Read them all!

# Just William

Read them all!

Just William

Read them all!

# Just William